To Co

'Share Your Gift'

12-25-05

To Squier.

'Share Shun Gift'

12-25-05

The Spirit of the Turquoise Necklace

The Schmooney Trilogies

By

Bob Shumaker

authorHOUSE™

1663 LIBERTY DRIVE, SUITE 200
BLOOMINGTON, INDIANA 47403
(800) 839-8640
WWW.AUTHORHOUSE.COM

First published by AuthorHouse 05/05/05

ISBN: 1-4208-5143-8 (sc)

Library of Congress Control Number: 2005903609

Printed in the United States of America
Bloomington, Indiana

This book is printed on acid-free paper.

Acknowledgments

A very special thank you to my wife of 28 years, Sharon, and to my daughter of 23 years, Katy, who gave me the opportunity to make this happen. I want to thank my family and all my friends for their continuous support, marvelous suggestions, and helpful ideas over the many years of developing this tale from a simple story into a trilogy. I also want to thank the management and staff at the Western North Carolina Nature Center in Asheville, North Carolina, for kindly sharing their fabulous facility and their immense knowledge. A special thank you to Griffin Campbell for his excellent cover art work and continuous support. A special thank you to my editor, Nancy Machlis Rechtman. And a special thank you to Kristan Swingle, for without her, this would have not been a reality.

Chapter 1

It was a warm June morning in Atlanta. Summer had finally arrived. I had been looking forward to it for months, not just because of the break from school, but because I would be spending it at Uncle Steve's house.

This particular June morning I was sitting on my bags in my room, reading a book about animals, while I waited for the rest of the family to finish packing for our visit with Uncle Steve. Ever since our trip to the mountains last spring, I had been reading about the animals in the forest.

I am always amazed at what animals can do and how they live. Animals are like people in many ways. For example, an American box turtle can live to be seventy years old. That's a really long time. In other ways, they're not so much like us. A box turtle travels at a rate of one mile per month. That is pretty slow when you compare that to our automobiles, which can travel up to two miles per minute. At the box turtle's pace, he sure doesn't go very fast or very far. I figured it would take him nearly his whole life just to travel from here to Disney World. Then I thought about it. I had been to Disney World and with some of those long lines, it would take him the rest of his life just to see Pirates of the Caribbean! I wondered whether the reason box turtles lived so long was that they just aren't in a hurry. There is not a lot of stress in your life when you take your time to do things. Maybe there was something for people to learn from box turtles?

Here is another fact I read: there are two hundred million insects for every human being on earth. Could that possibly be right? I was thinking about that very fact when I heard, "Hey, Austin, Dad says you're holding us up!"

That was Katie, my little sister. She was going to Uncle Steve's house with me for two reasons. The first reason was that taking Katie was the only way I was getting permission to go. Can you say "compromise?" The second reason was that, although she was an eight-year-old girl, she wasn't that bad...as sisters go. Yeah, she whined, played with dolls and did stupid things. But then again, she could keep a secret. And that's not bad, as little sisters go.

I went back to reading my book. I wanted to find one more interesting fact. Did you know that humans are the only animals to sleep on their backs? Well, I didn't. The book said so, but I was not so sure. I had seen my uncle's cat, Franklin, sleep in every position possible: on his back, on his side, and twisted just about any way you could imagine. I'd seen him sleeping on a window ledge that was no more that than four inches across. And once I found him sound asleep lying across one of the arms of a chair. I thought he was dead. I touched his back. He didn't move. I touched his head. He still didn't move. I was getting worried; I liked this cat. I grabbed some hair on his back and began to pull it. He suddenly woke up, leaped straight up in the air, and jumped to the floor. It scared me so much I screamed. Then I let go of his hair. I bet it scared him, too.

"Austin, we're leaving in five minutes, with you or without you."

That was my dad. He's serious when he says things like that. I knew I had better get moving.

The plan was for me to stay with Uncle Steve for the entire summer. Two months in Mountview - it was going to be great. Katie was coming with me, but only for four weeks. I figured that I could endure anything for four weeks, especially since I would have the rest of the summer in Mountview without her.

Two months away from home requires some serious packing. I was sitting on one of my two duffel bags. The red and black one with the Atlanta Hawks logo on it was the one I had packed. It held my survival gear – a must up in the Appalachian Mountains – along with my Georgia Tech sweatshirt, my Georgia Tech hat, a pair of jeans, hiking boots, underwear, and a pair of socks. I even threw in toothpaste, toothbrush, some deodorant, and my dad's old razor. After all, I was twelve.

The second bag was what my mom packed after she saw what I had put into the first bag. It held lots more underwear, socks, handkerchiefs, new jeans, clean shirts, running shoes, two sweaters, and summer reading for school – as if Mountview needed more books. I would take that bag because I had to, but there wasn't any way that I was going to need all that stuff. After all, I was only going to be gone for two months!

The trip to Uncle Steve's house usually took about two hours. We had been going to Mountview at least once a year for my whole life, so we had developed a routine that was almost a ritual. New things happened from time to time, but the basic pattern never changed. I won't bore you by repeating all the details, but the trip did have its moments.

One of my favorite things to do while traveling was playing "Name-That-Animal," the game that Dad came up a long time ago as a way to keep us quiet and challenge our minds. Dad always found ways to remind us to use our creativity.

"Name-That-Animal" is a fun game to play. Here's how it works. You take a box of animal crackers and give out all the crackers so that each player has the same amount. Then each player has ten minutes to create their very own strange creature and name it. Each player takes body parts from different animals by gnawing off the pieces of the cracker that they don't want to keep. For example, if I have a lion and decide to keep the head, then I would eat everything but the head and place the head on a paper towel. Next I might have an elephant. So I would eat the elephant except for, say, the trunk. Next I might have a giraffe. I would eat everything but his neck. Next I would eat the horse but save its legs. The key was precision biting. And here is the best part – you got to eat all the crackers, with the exception of the animal parts that you needed to save, and then at the end of the game you ate those parts too. Plus, nobody yelled at you about the crumbs. What could beat that?

Another highlight of our trip was the place where once Mom puked. Katie never let us miss that. She could be doing something else that had her complete attention, but somehow she would stop at the very moment we were passing that particular spot and say, "Hey, that's where Mom puked," and point to the side of the road. I had seen her do it without even raising her head. That had amazed me. As I said, Katie wasn't too bad, as eight-year-old sisters go.

Despite the usual stuff, I suspected the trip that morning was going to be different. Why, you ask? The main reason was that I would be staying up there, without my parents, for a long time. I knew Mom and Dad would want to give me last minute advice about that. Also, Katie would be with me for the first four weeks and I would be responsible for her, so Mom and Dad would want to give me last minute advice about that, too. And I would have my first real job, working at the Nature Museum, so Mom and Dad would give me last minute advice about that, too. If you added up all the last minute advice, I was afraid they would talk non-stop all the way to Mountview.

Our trip started out just as it usually did. Before I knew it, we were already through the Atlanta traffic and headed up I-85. We were halfway to Commerce by the time Dad was done thinking about the details of the trip and all the things he forgot to do before we left. It was time for him to break the silence. But my mom beat him to it.

"Austin," she began, "are you excited about your vacation?"

That was the first time that anyone had referred to my adventure as a vacation. But Mom was right; it would be a vacation even though I was going to be working at the Nature Museum. "Yes ma'am, I am."

"We're going to miss you two," she said, directing her comments to both of us while she reached back and patted Katie's knee.

"I'll miss you too, Mommy," Katie responded.

Dad jumped in. "Austin, are you comfortable with all of this? Is there anything that you would like to discuss?"

"I'm fine with it," I answered. As I thought about it, I knew that was true. I tried to come up with reasons, but I couldn't think how to explain it. Then I remembered summer camp and thought that this would be the same as camp. "You know, last year's camp was the longest I was away from home, until this. I was fine with that. I'll be fine with this, Dad."

I had spent four weeks the previous summer at Camp-Y-Noah, where the counselors had taught me and my fellow campers to paddle a canoe, eat dehydrated food and live in tents. Then we had camped out for a whole week while we paddled the Chattooga River. It was a great experience. Although that special YMCA camping trip was usually reserved for thirteen and fourteen-year-olds, a letter my Uncle Steve sent to the YMCA staff had helped me receive special permission to attend. Apparently, Steven Cook had some pull at the YMCA. He had explained that when it came to the outdoors, I was far more mature than my age indicated. Uncle Steve would know, because he was the one who had taught me.

4

My dad continued. "You'll have more responsibility this year. You will have Katie to watch over. You will have a job at the Nature Museum. And you will need to mind Uncle Steve and Amy. Those are all big things to consider."

When I considered all my 'responsibilities,' I began wondering why I was going. It was to have fun, wasn't it? But I had expected the last minute advice, so I said, "Yes sir, I know."

"I have something here for you, Austin," Mom said as she retrieved a small piece of paper from her purse. She held the paper in her hand, put her purse on the car seat next to her, then turned around to look at me. "I know you were expecting to get some last-minute advice. That's what parents do to try to help you make good decisions. But instead of lecturing, I thought that I would write something down for you to carry with you, as a reminder to do the right thing. Here it is." She handed me the paper.

I opened it and read what it said. Then I looked up at her.

"Read it out loud," she said.

I read, "'Behavior is how you act when everyone is watching. Character is how you act when no one is watching.'" I looked up at Mom again. "What does it mean?"

"It means that I know you will be on your best behavior; you always are. But being good is about more than behaving well. It's also about building character – that's what life is all about. You build character when you do the right thing even when no one is checking up on you. So all I ask is that you think about your character whenever you need to make a decision about what to do. OK?"

"Sure, Mom," I replied. I folded the scrap of paper and slipped it into my pocket.

I noticed that there was a fly on the inside of my window. He was standing there looking at me. Or maybe he was looking through the window wondering why he couldn't get out. I opened the window slowly. He didn't move. I opened it some more, then cupped my hand over him to push him out the window. Then he was gone. I figured that if there were two hundred million insects for just one of me then I didn't want to make him, or his two hundred million friends, mad.

5

It was Dad's turn again. He said, "Austin, I know that you are interested in learning more about your telepathic ability. I know you believe there is something to all of that. Your mother and I just don't know. All I ask is that you don't get too excited about something that may not be there. I don't want you to get your hopes up, just to be let down. Let nature take its course, and take all of this a little at a time. OK?"

Dad was cool about this. He and Mom were aware that something had happened up in Mountview over Spring break, but Amy, Uncle Steve, Dr. Dixon, myself, and even Katie – I told you she could keep a secret – had kept the details to ourselves. It was better that way, at least until we had a chance to figure it out. "Yes, sir," I agreed, "let nature take its course."

I looked over and saw that Katie was still playing with her dolls. The blonde one was getting a new hairdo and the red-haired one was in need of some pants. Our car slowed down. We were turning onto State Route 33.

Mom asked, "Do we have time for a game?"

Katie was into her dolls and didn't even hear the question, or she perhaps was just ignoring Mom – both very good possibilities. I said, "Before we do that, I have a question. What exactly does 'Let nature take its course' mean?"

Dad spoke first. "I can help you there." He paused, collected his thoughts, and then he used his teacher voice. "I believe that a quote from Benjamin Disraeli might help answer that question."

I knew I shouldn't have asked.

"Disraeli said, 'Nature is more powerful than education; time will develop everything.' It means that you shouldn't force things to happen; if it goes against nature then it may happen, but it won't last."

Dad stayed focused on driving, but I had noticed that sometimes while he was speaking he would glance out the side window, like he was gathering his thoughts. Or maybe he thought he was back in class and he was practicing scanning the room, as if he was looking at all the students. This time, he glanced at me in the rear view mirror before continuing.

"Nature always has the advantage of time. Nature developed things before we arrived on earth and nature will continue to develop things after we have all departed from earth. The quote says, 'Time will develop everything.' So, 'Let nature take its course' is the same as saying, 'Ours is not to control nature but to work with her, allowing for natural evolution over time.' Does that make sense?"

It did make sense, but before I could answer, Mom jumped in. She turned around to look at me and said thoughtfully, "I believe the quote suggests that nature has a plan for us. We can alter that plan by changing nature. But nature has a way of reclaiming what was rightfully hers. So it is better to let nature determine her path, and it is better for us to leave her alone. What do you think about that interpretation?"

"Not bad," Dad said.

"I think I understand," I said.

I did think it made some sense that 'Let nature take its course' was about letting things happen by themselves. Nature is a powerful force and we should work with her. But I was on overload from my parents' complicated answers to my question. I had been hoping for a quick and easy answer.

After thinking it over for a moment, I said, "Now I have another question: Why do we call it Mother Nature and Father Time - why not Father Nature and Mother Time?"

That stopped the conversation in its tracks. I'm still waiting for *that* answer.

I looked out my window and noticed that we had reached the winding roads that led up the mountains. As we had learned over the years, you didn't read, write or draw while you were on this part of the trip. Maybe that's why Mom and Dad didn't answer me. Dad was now totally focused on navigating the twisting road and Mom was totally focused on not repeating her barfing performance - the one that Katie would not let her forget. I could see that special bend in the road up ahead; we were almost there. I looked over at Katie. Her blonde head was still bent over her dolls. She impatiently brushed a stray curl out of her eyes as she finally put pants on the red-haired one.

Without looking up, Katie said, "Hey, that's where Mom puked!"

I briefly heard Mom commenting to Katie on her lack of manners, but since Mom couldn't turn around without feeling sick, most of her words were lost to the roar of the engine.

Katie never did look up. I wondered how she did it.

I lowered my window to let the fresh air soothe my face and settle my stomach, which is always a good thing to do when you are in the back seat of a car on a curvy road. Winding roads really mess with your stomach. My mom's reaction was proof of that. I mean, while your body shifts from one side of your seat to the other, moving to the left as the car turns right, then moving to the right as the car turns left, then left, then right – you get the picture – fresh air is really important. Plus the last thing I want to hear is Katie saying, 'Look, that's where Austin puked.'

I eased my arm onto the window's edge, directing the cool mountain breeze against my face. With my eyes closed and the breeze flowing across my face, I could dream of being an Olympic skier or a NASCAR driver, or of soaring in a hang glider high above the Cliffs of Glassy – anything I wanted to be or do. But I was not dreaming of any of those things. Instead, I was thinking of Sarah.

I had been thinking about Sarah a lot since I left Mountview two months before. She had been one of the hardest secrets to keep, but Katie and I had managed it. I wished I had heard news from Amy. Thinking of that reminded me of Dr. Dixon. I moved my other arm so that my fingers could touch the pocket where I kept the letter he had sent to me after my visit last spring. I was looking forward to seeing him again.

Dad was slowing the car as we approached Mountview's only traffic light. The light was red, which gave me time to look out the window where I could see downtown Mountview, all four marvelous blocks of it. There were some people walking around but, with several parking spaces empty on both sides, I could tell that it was still a little early for this sleepy little town. The town would be a lot busier in another hour.

The light turned green and we moved on. We were almost at Uncle Steve's house.

Uncle Steve's house was built back from the road. The driveway curved slightly through several large trees on the way from the road to the front walk and beyond, to the garage. The front yard wasn't really a yard like we had at home; it was 'natural.' The woods came right up to the house on both sides, as if the house had been lifted up and dropped right in the middle of all the trees.

The front door opened and Uncle Steve walked out with Amy following close behind. Then Edison lumbered out behind them, pushing past their legs to race toward the car. Uncle Steve looked about the same as the last time I had seen him, except he appeared to be a bit heavier. His denim shirt was just a little tight. Amy must have been cooking for him. Amy was as slim and pretty as ever. Of course, she was used to her own cooking. She caught up to Uncle Steve and said something that made him laugh, then she turned to us with a big smile on her face. I guess she was really happy to see us.

I was eager to see Uncle Steve, Edison and Franklin. But most of all, I was anxious to talk to Amy. She was the last person who had seen Sarah. They had planned to stay in touch over these last two months. However, Amy had sent me a letter telling me that she had only seen Sarah once. So, although I would say hello to everyone, I really wanted to get Amy alone to ask her if she had any news about Sarah.

Let me take a moment and tell you about Sarah. Sarah is a skunk who I first met during my last trip to Uncle Steve's, which was last spring. Sarah was burned during a forest fire and Amy, who runs the Nature Center, found Sarah and helped her recover. I met Sarah at Amy's Nature Center and, after Sarah recovered, Amy, Uncle Steve, and I let Sarah loose, back into the forest. Then Sarah came to visit me at Uncle Steve's. And that was when things really got interesting. See, I have this gift. We all have gifts that we are born with. Well, my gift is the ability to communicate with animals. Sarah has a similar ability. I know she is an animal and I know this sounds really strange. Believe me, it is strange. But she and I can carry on a conversation by 'sending.' Sending is like talking to someone who is not near you, like in another room or in another house. I can speak out loud and Sarah can hear me from far away. It is like we both have a built-in telephone. Sarah can 'send' me a message and I can hear her. Unfortunately, at that time, I had to speak out loud when I 'sent' her a message. So it sounded pretty weird when someone else was near me, because they would think I was either talking to them, or talking to myself. Usually they thought I was crazy. Crazy? You know I just might have been crazy. All of that happened so quickly that I was really beginning to wonder back then. However, then I met Dr. Dixon, Mountview's resident authority on those things, who assured me that this 'gift,' which is a form of telepathy, was a good thing and really something to study. He understood that this was weird and helped me through it. I will tell you more about it as this story developed.

When I opened my car door I was startled to find Edison right there. Before I could get the seatbelt off, he stuck his head in the car, almost banging me in the face. He looked like he had a big grin on his face and his tongue was hanging out. Before I could stop him, he tried to get his whole body in the back seat with me. I blocked him with my arms and laughed as he braced his front paws on my lap, shoved his big black head against me and licked my face. Edison was a large dog, but he wasn't that heavy. Uncle Steve has described Edison as a 'lightweight' because although he looked big, it was mostly all of his fur that made him seem so big.

"Hey, Edison, whoa boy, there's no room for you in here!" I pushed him back out of the car, then sat on the corner of the seat and rubbed his head. I knew he was excited to see me and wanted to play. "Not just yet, big boy, after lunch."

He heard Katie outside the car and ran to see her. He must have started licking her because I heard Katie squealing from behind the car, "Edison, eeewwwwww!"

After the customary greetings, Dad gave me the heaviest bag to carry while he and Uncle Steve gathered up the rest. As soon as I walked in the front door, Franklin started rubbing against my legs. I looked down and saw the big bundle of gray fur circling my leg, coming back for another rub. I set my bag down and picked up the old boy.

"Hey Franklin, how's my boy?"

Franklin was doing fine. He seemed to have gained some weight since spring. Maybe Amy was cooking for him, too. I rubbed his head in all the right places. Franklin appreciated my greeting with the total enjoyment cats are so good at. After he felt comfortable knowing that I was all right, he wanted down to greet Katie.

I could smell lunch. Amy and Uncle Steve had prepared a roasted chicken and it smelled delicious. As soon as we had taken our bags to our rooms, we all met on the deck to eat. I spotted platters of chicken and Stove Top stuffing on the big round table, shaded from the midday sun by the table's umbrella. There was also a bowl of green stuff that looked like a salad, but there were some strange things in it.

Who had ever heard of a salad with orange slices on top? I looked at it and put a little on my plate. The lettuce was crisp but the orange slice was slimy. I moved it around my plate with my fork. The orange slice reminded me of a slug that you find in the garden. Then the lettuce reminded me of the plants in the garden. Then I thought of eating a plant with a slug on it and couldn't get that thought out of my mind. I glanced over at Katie and she was staring at her salad, too. Based on the expression on her face, Katie was making the same comparison. I spread the small amount of salad around my plate, to make it look like I had eaten a lot of it and just hadn't bothered to scrape the remaining pieces into a pile. Then I dove into the chicken and stuffing. It tasted great. I wondered whose idea it was to put slugs in the salad.

The lunch conversation was your standard grownup discussion. Katie and I had heard it all before. Dad and Uncle Steve talked about current events. Dad talked about the courses he would be taking that summer at Georgia State University. Uncle Steve talked about land development in the area. Mom talked about visiting my Grandma Betty in Florida and what she was going to wear. Amy listened intently to all of them. When there was a break in the conversation she commented that the Nature Museum had played a part in recent local events.

I listened a little more closely. Amy explained that a year ago, the state had detected low levels of some harmful chemicals in nearby waterways. Then last month, after someone had brought a sick raccoon to the Nature Museum with high levels of toxins in its system, Amy had notified the proper government authorities. When the state retested the water, they found that the levels of harmful substances had increased over the last year. Many people were concerned, but so far the investigators had not been able to locate the source.

I thought again about Sarah. How could I get a chance to ask Amy about her? I decided to wait until after lunch and then ask Amy to go on a hike. I needed to get her alone, but with this crowd, it wasn't going to be easy. How was I going to shake Uncle Steve? I had only one card to play. I decided to play it now.

"So, Uncle Steve, are you going to help Katie with her summer project?" I asked, as we carried our dishes into the kitchen.

Uncle Steve looked over at Katie and said, "Sure I will. What kind of project do you have, Katie?"

Katie glared at me. Doing school work was not what she wanted to think about on her first day at Uncle Steve's. That was OK; she'd get over it.

"My summer project is about animals," she said. "I have to make a list of the animals that I see this summer and write a paragraph about each one. If I do well, then I'll get an 'A' for my project grade for the first semester next year."

"Well, you've come to the right place to do that," Uncle Steve told her.

That was my opening. "Uncle Steve, maybe Katie could set up her work area in your office."

"Sure," he said. "Sounds good to me. Katie, you and I will go upstairs and do just that." He ruffled her curls and waited politely for her to stand. "After you, my dear," he said, escorting her from the room.

It couldn't have worked better.

"Amy," I said, "would you like to go for a walk while Uncle Steve helps Katie with her project?"

And just like that, it was set. Not bad. Mom would clean the table and put away the food; Dad would read the local paper. He liked to do that. Amy and I would go for a short walk. I figured it would be just long enough for me to get all the details I wanted about Sarah.

Chapter 2

Amy and I went out the back door, crossed the deck, and then walked down the path into the woods. Amy's long, straight hair moved slightly in the breeze as she walked. Her hair was almost black, much darker than mine. Her skin was darker too, even when she didn't have a suntan. The day was warming as the sun peeked through broken clouds. The air was full of wonderful smells and you could hear the treetops fluttering in the breeze. This was another beautiful day in Mountview.

We took the path that led toward the creek. We were barely out of sight from the house when I asked, "So, where is she? How is Sarah?"

Amy stopped and turned to face me. "Austin, gosh, how did I know you were going to ask me that?" she asked jokingly. She smiled, then continued more seriously. "As I told you in my letter, Sarah only visited me once. It was about a week after you left. I haven't seen her since."

We walked on, and Amy told me about their one encounter. "Sarah was at the back door. I heard her scratching on the screen and went to the door. She looked exactly the same, still sporting the tag in her ear. She came by with a friend, as if she just wanted to say hi. They were both sniffing around. All seemed well."

Amy could see that I was troubled by Sarah's long absence. "Maybe she found a boyfriend. Spring can be like that, you know," Amy said gently.

"No, not for Sarah; she wouldn't do that to me!" I exclaimed.

"She wouldn't do what to you, Austin?"

"You know, do that without telling me," I replied without thinking.

"Oh, you mean have *another* boyfriend?"

When Amy emphasized 'another,' I realized I was going down a road that I did not want to go down. She was right. I was jealous. Why was I jealous? Jealous of what? I needed to change the subject.

"No, not that at all. I guess I'm worried about her, that's all."

"It's all right to be worried," Amy agreed. "I must admit that I am a little worried myself. But we have to remember that we are dealing with an animal. An animal, I might add, that no one knows much about. So who is to say what is normal? Perhaps this is normal. Let's not worry," she suggested.

"You're right, I'm sure she's fine," I said, suddenly relieved that this conversation I had been so eager for was over.

What I had said without thinking was the way I felt. I knew it was true. But what was I feeling? I didn't know. This was confusing.

We continued down the path, watching nature at her best. The trees and bushes were rustling with life and birds were singing. The familiar sights, sounds and smells of the forest soothed my worries.

Amy was walking quietly beside me when she touched my arm and said softly, "Listen!"

We stopped walking. Both of us directed our attention to the sounds around us. I listened for something out of the ordinary. We moved our heads slowly, hoping for more volume or to isolate a clearer sound. Have you ever noticed how people move their heads around to try to pick up sounds, just like animals do? Except animals also can move their ears. I always thought that humans got short-changed when it came to ears. Wouldn't it be cool to be able to move our ears around like a dog moves its ears? When Edison hears something weird, his ears can move in all sorts of directions. Can you imagine what we would be like if our ears moved like that?

I was thinking of that when Amy said, "Let's call Dr. Dixon when we get back, and go see him tomorrow. Sarah said he knew more than he let on. Perhaps he can tell us whether we should be concerned."

I turned to look at Amy, "Was *that* what you wanted us to listen for?"

Amy grinned. "No, but I saw that smile on your face and figured you were off somewhere else anyway."

"Oh. I was just thinking about what it would be like if people had dog ears," I admitted.

"Sure, Austin. What would you like, Beagle or Doberman?"

"I was thinking about the way dogs direct their ears when…"

"Wait, there it is again, did you hear it?" Amy interrupted. "Can you hear the crows in the distance? That should be a very familiar sound to you."

She was right. I remembered it well from the last time I had been there.

Amy said, "Let's move in that direction and see what they're so excited about."

The noise led us east, to a path I hadn't been on for a long time. Now I could plainly hear the sounds of several crows. The sounds were getting louder. I could hear several 'caws' from different directions, just ahead. I followed Amy around a bend in the trail and saw that the forest opened up into a large clearing.

"Cawww, cawwww, cawwww." Now instead of two caws together, we were getting it in threes. They were long, loud notes. Again we heard the call, coming from several different crows, all having something to say. The sound was getting louder.

We stopped walking, Amy pointed to a spot near the edge of the clearing where we crouched down to make ourselves less noticeable. Two crows were hopping around something on the ground. I couldn't tell exactly what it was, but back home we would have called it road-kill. When the loud caws came again, I was surprised to discover that the crows on the ground weren't the ones making the noises; the noises were coming from the trees above.

Amy turned toward me and spoke very quietly. "These might be the same crows that helped us last spring. See them?" She pointed into the trees. "Those crows are lookouts for the crows that are having lunch. Next time, or later in this meal, the crows will change positions and the lookouts will then get their meal. It works that way with many of the animals in the forest."

"Crows are smarter than we think, aren't they?" I observed.

"Austin, all animals are instinctively smarter than most people imagine. I don't really know about smarter, but their instincts have been developed over centuries. It would be safe to say that we should never underestimate the instinctive intelligence of an animal. They have gotten by for a long time without our help. If we'd just respect animals' homes and lives, we could all live in harmony."

Uncle Steve had told us the same thing for years, but this helped me understand it better.

The cawing continued, long, loud notes. "Cawww, cawww, cawww."

Amy turned her head to watch the crows for a moment before continuing. "Crows are clever, alert birds. They do not have musical voices. However, that cawing you hear is just one of about twenty calls they use to communicate with each other."

"You mean they have their own language?" I asked, amazed.

"Yes, they do."

We watched the crows move around on the ground. "See how they walk? Their feet are strong, which makes them well adapted for walking."

"How smart can they be? If I had wings, I wouldn't do a lot of walking," I said smartly.

"If you had wings, we all would be in trouble."

I wasn't sure exactly what she meant by that comment, but I thought it would be best to move to another subject. So I said, "If crows are this smart, then owls must really be smart."

Amy turned to me and smiled. "Actually, crows are considered the most intelligent of birds; even smarter than owls. I read about a documented case where they tested the intelligence of the crow. A crow was in a cage that was about four inches above a table." She used her finger and thumb to show me how high that was. "They placed food on the table, right under the cage but out of the crow's reach. Then they put a straight piece of wire in the cage. The crow took the wire in his beak and bent it into a 'J' shape. Then he held the straight end in his beak and with the hook end, 'hooked' the food and pulled it into his cage so he could eat it. Pretty smart, don't you think?"

"Wow!" I said, and looked back at the crow pulling a piece of meat off the 'road kill.' It was time for something funny, so I said, "And I didn't even know that crows knew our alphabet."

Amy groaned.

We stood up and started back down the path, leaving the crows to their lunch. They quieted down as we distanced ourselves from them.

After a time, Amy returned to our earlier conversation. "So, let's go see Dr. Dixon tomorrow. You and I can go into town after breakfast. Are you up for a visit to Bevin's Candy Store?"

"That sounds great. Sure, let's go see Dr. Dixon tomorrow. He wrote me a letter. I've been wanting to talk with him."

"A letter? Do you mind telling me what he said?" she asked.

"He said this 'gift' that I have needs to be taken seriously…that I shouldn't talk about it with others, at least until we know more about it. He also said that this Schmooney stuff should be kept quiet until we know more about that, too."

"He's right, Austin. You do have a special gift. I don't know what it is, exactly, but it is special." She looked as if she wanted to say something else but was trying to figure out how to say it.

"We each like to do certain things," she continued after a moment. "The things we like to do, we usually do better than things we don't like to do. Some of us develop special skills in certain things that we like to do. The special skills we develop become our talents. You have heard someone being referred to as 'talented,' right?"

"Sure," I replied. Amy stopped walking and turned to look at me.

"Some people, like you, have talents that they haven't developed. We call those natural talents, or raw talents, since they came naturally rather than being skills that grew because they were things you liked to do. You need to take the time to develop your natural talents. You have been given those skills for a reason."

This was odd, I thought. I had heard this before. She watched me, waiting for me to say something. I took a deep breath, then shared what I hadn't told anyone else.

"That is exactly what Dr. Dixon told me in his letter. He said he wanted to see me when I got back here so we could discuss it further. He also said I shouldn't be afraid, that all of this was a good thing."

Amy smiled, seeming very pleased that she and Dr. Dixon had offered me the same advice. "Well, they say great minds think alike."

We walked the rest of the way to the house in silence. I was looking forward to learning more, but I wasn't ready to talk about it anymore just then.

When we reached the deck, Dad and Uncle Steve were getting ready to leave to see the old family property. Katie was working on her summer project in Uncle Steve's office. Amy ended up in the library with Mom, talking about local crafts.

So what was I going to do next? Things had been moving fast since I got here. If that continued, it was going to be a very busy summer.

* * * * *

It was going to be a busy summer for Harvey Gaines, too. What I would learn later was at that very moment, Harvey was standing on the western shore of Lake Minti staring out into the beautiful, calm blue waters of that remote mountain stream-fed retreat.

Lake Minti, located on the border between North and South Carolina, had a reputation for being one of the cleanest and clearest lakes in the Carolinas. It looked pristine. Unfortunately, the state's environmental tests had shown that if you ate largemouth or spotted bass from the lake you would be consuming mercury, a toxic metal that can cause severe neurological problems.

The mercury in Lake Minti had risen from trace amounts to a dangerous level in just one year. The state had issued a warning about Lake Minti that spring. They had distributed 60,000 copies of an advisory to bait and tackle shops, landings, convenience stores, and anyone else who called for information.

Harvey knew what would happen if he, and others dedicated to finding the source, didn't come up with answers soon. He was very worried. In fact, he thought about it all the time.

Chapter 3

I heard Dad and Uncle Steve talking. That's what woke me up. I was sitting in the big red leather chair in the library where I had fallen asleep. I had been reading one of Uncle Steve's many books, *The Count of Monte Cristo*. I thought about what I had read. I was at the part where Dantes follows the treasure map given to him by his friend, the priest. He finds the exact spot marked on the map and then uncovers the chest of precious stones.

I had no idea what time it was. Like many of the rooms in Uncle Steve's house, this was a room without a clock.

Dad noticed that I was awake. "Hey, partner, it's almost time for dinner. How's the book?"

I gathered my thoughts, shaking the sleep from my head. "The book is exciting. What time is it, Dad?"

"About 6 o'clock," he told me. "You've been asleep for a couple of hours. Why don't you wash your hands and meet us in the kitchen?"

Dinner consisted of Dad's excellent hamburgers. When you added Vernors ginger ale and Fritos corn chips, the meal became a feast. Katie and I dug into our food and let the adults carry on the dinner conversation.

It began with Dad saying, "I can't believe that they will allow them to do that. I just can't believe it."

Mom asked, "What are you talking about, Ben?"

Dad explained. After visiting the family property, he and Uncle Steve had gone into town, where Dad had learned that one of the local developers was planning to build a fifteen-story condominium right on top of a mountain.

"Do you know what that will look like?" he asked angrily. "It will look like crap!"

Silence fell over the dinner table, as everyone stared at my dad and then quickly looked away. I knew he had sworn before, but very seldom had he said those kinds of words in front of us kids. I know what you are thinking - 'crap' isn't a very bad word. And I agree with you. I had heard a lot worse at school, and that was just from the teachers, when they thought there weren't any kids around. But Dad had a rule about cuss words. He always said that if your vocabulary was so limited that you had to use those words, then you didn't have much worth saying anyway. I guess he had a point. Anyway, we all just looked at each other in disbelief. 'My dad must really be raging,' was what I was thinking. Raging was 'the' new word that kids had been using around school. I think it meant that someone was really angry. Anyone could pick up a whole new vocabulary just by listening to what other kids said. Anyhow, raging was 'the' new word and raging was what my Dad was doing at this time.

"Wow, you are really raging," Uncle Steve said.

There was a pause, giving Uncle Steve's words time to settle. Then the whole room erupted in laughter. Dad laughed, too.

"I'm sorry," he said, "but I just can't believe that the Town Council would allow anyone to chop off the top of a mountain, a beautiful mountain, and plop fifteen stories of brick and mortar there. That is shameless. It's horrible. Somebody needs to do something about it. Steve, can you imagine what our father would say about that?"

"I think he would be as upset as you are, Ben. But there is time yet," Uncle Steve responded. "These types of things take time and there are procedures that must be followed. Those procedures are designed as protective measures."

I jumped in. "Are they really going to put a building on a mountain-top?"

Amy answered, "So far, they are just talking about it. Nothing has been approved yet."

"Talking about it?" Dad objected. "I just saw the plans in town. The real estate agents are drooling at the mere idea of it."

Mom said quietly, "Ben, you knew it was just a matter of time before Mountview would be developed."

"I know you're right," Dad said a little more calmly. "But you should build *with* the environment, not against it. Mountview has always been built with the environment. Brick and mortar don't belong on the top of a mountain. Maybe people do that in other places, but not in Mountview."

"There is a town meeting Tuesday night," Amy volunteered. "Everyone who attends that can present their opinions."

"I wish that I was going to be here," Dad said. "Steve, you and Amy have to present some logic to this community. They are thinking like crazy people."

"Ben, nothing is going to happen. At least not until all sides have been presented," Uncle Steve reassured Dad. "Remember, this community has preserved Mountview for a long time; it will be preserved for a lot longer. Don't worry."

"Can you imagine what the Indians must be thinking?" Dad asked, shaking his head. "There goes the neighborhood."

"Can you imagine what the community is thinking?" Uncle Steve responded. "This will be one big dogfight."

I spoke up again. "They can't butcher the mountain just for a building, can they?"

"Not without a fight," Dad agreed. "Our ancestors didn't spend their lives fighting to preserve this land just to see it get paved over so some developer can make a fortune."

"What's worse, they are planning to build it near Sunset Rock," Amy informed them.

"What? That's one of the most popular places for hiking. Why, we have had several picnics there ourselves," Mom observed.

"More importantly," Amy added, "there are several Indian burial grounds on that property. The Park Service and the local tribes are very concerned about that."

This discussion lasted through dinner and then continued in the library, where we gathered around the fireplace. All that talking left everyone ready for an early bedtime. After my nap I was not terribly sleepy, but I was too disturbed by the reckless development plans to want to stay up. Katie and I went upstairs and got ready for bed. She was asleep as soon as her head hit her pillow. I tossed and turned for awhile. My thoughts bounced back and forth between Sarah and the building project. I kept thinking about the natural landscape being changed forever, and it got me even more upset.

When sleep finally came, I drifted deep into a dream. Maybe it was sparked by the day's events or perhaps it was my grandfather, who shared a bit of my soul, sending me a message. Or maybe it was someone in another dimension, trying to speak to me. No one really knows what triggers dreams. Whatever the source, that dream was about to deliver a message that would change my life forever.

In my dream, I was walking along a country road. I could see the road curving up ahead. The day was clear and sunny. Beautiful evergreens covered the land on both sides of the road, casting long shadows on the blacktop. I was wearing a uniform, one with a green shirt and green pants. I realized that I wasn't just walking; I was working. I worked for the state and I was cleaning the road, sweeping dirt and grass off to the side. I was working on the edge of the highway, where the asphalt met the ground. Although I could not see anyone else around me, I did not have the feeling of being alone. Everything seemed peaceful and safe. I was content just doing my job, cleaning the road.

As I swept gravel, dirt and cut grass off the pavement, something caught my attention. There was something sticking out of the asphalt just ahead of me. Wanting a better look, I knelt down on one knee. I could now see that what was pushing out of the asphalt appeared to be fingertips, and that the fingertips seemed to be attached to something under the blacktop. Oddly, this didn't alarm me. I still felt safe, but I knew that there was something more to discover.

I began to brush away the remaining dirt and grass. An image began to appear just below the asphalt. My hands were now moving very fast.

The image was growing clearer and clearer. A face and a body, directly below me, beneath the asphalt. I dropped to my hands and knees, working feverishly to clear the remaining debris. Then it appeared. I froze in disbelief, staring at the image. It was a beautiful girl with bronzed skin and long black hair, wearing traditional Indian garb. An Indian princess? She certainly looked like an Indian princess. Her arms were extended above her head. I followed them and saw that it was her outstretched fingers that had first caught my attention.

Suddenly, she turned her head and her dark eyes met mine. I fell back in amazement and shock as she sat upright. The asphalt fell away from her in chunks. There we were, staring at each other. She was dressed in a soft deerskin dress and a beautifully beaded headband. But what was most noticeable was the turquoise and silver necklace around her neck. Its elaborate central pendant was formed in the shape of an animal. Although its features seemed somehow familiar, I knew that I had never seen such an animal before. The necklace glistened and flashed in the sunlight. It almost seemed to glow from within, capturing my complete attention until I was barely aware of anything else. Then she spoke, breaking the spell.

"Austin?" She said my name. *How did she know my name?* My eyes moved back to her face. She looked at me directly, locking her eyes with mine. "Austin, we need your help. Help us, please." And, with that, she reached out and gently touched my face.

I rocketed out of my deep, trancelike dream, sitting straight up in my bed, gasping for air. My fingers slowly moved to my right cheek where her hand had touched me. It had seemed so real. Still sorting out the details, I gradually became aware of my surroundings. I looked around, reassured by the familiar sight of my bedroom at Uncle Steve's house. I was safe; I was home. Then I noticed Katie standing next to my bed, staring at me. I must have made so much noise that I had awakened her.

I said, "Boy, am I glad you are here. Listen to this..." and began to tell her about my dream. Occasionally, I glanced away to gather my thoughts, but mostly I watched Katie, who was listening intently. I told her about the work detail, the fingers, and then about wiping away the debris on the asphalt and seeing the image below. As I described the Indian princess, Katie started to smile. Later, I remembered thinking how odd it was for Katie to stand quietly for so long.

Her expression slowly changed. No, it was more than that. I stopped talking and watched, my eyes riveted on her. Katie's hair looked darker. And it was getting longer! Her face was changing! My mouth dropped open in amazement, but, once again, I was not afraid. As she reached out and touched my face, I noticed the turquoise necklace. My eyes widened. I looked again at her face. It wasn't Katie any more at all. It was the Indian princess!

My eyes were fixed on hers, in total disbelief. Her right hand was still touching my cheek. Out of instinct, my right arm began to rise. My arm slowly extended and I reached out my fingers to touch her shoulder. Expecting to feel her dress, I was surprised when my hand felt nothing. I extended my arm farther and farther. Nothing. My hand passed completely through her body, which was now drifting across the floor.

I could still feel her touch against my cheek as she spoke again, "Austin, we need your help. Please, please help us."

I watched in awe as the increasingly cloudy image that was once Katie floated across the table and out through the window. The image disappeared. It was replaced by the sight of Katie in her bed, fast asleep. But not for long.

"KATIE!" I yelled. And with that, reality returned.

Chapter 4

The morning sun found me fast asleep in my bedroom. I was awakened in my favorite way, by the smell of breakfast cooking, the fresh summer air flowing in through the window, and birds chirping in the background. I looked at the ceiling, idly watching the pattern of sunlight and shadows, while random thoughts entered my head. What a dream, I recalled. I noticed that Katie was still in bed – that was nothing new. I got up, pulled the covers over the bed and grabbed my stuff. I put on my favorite Georgia Tech sweatshirt, jeans, and my socks and boots. I did my customary check in the mirror – no white stuff, no boogers, and my hair was OK, too. The summer sun was starting to make my hair a lighter color. The sun does that. My mom told me that the sun bleaches hair and makes it change color. So I stood there looking at my hair, wondering what I would look like if I was blonde. I moved my head from side to side, examining each side as if I had long, blonde hair like Katie. Then I thought what I would look like if I was bald, like Mr. Kleiner, my math teacher. Oh no! I didn't want to think about that any longer. I rechecked myself; I looked all right. I heard Katie begin to stir, so I quietly left the bathroom and closed the bedroom door behind me.

I ran down the stairs and heard familiar sounds from the kitchen. The door-that-opens-both-ways was already open and I saw Mom and Dad at the table.

"Good morning," I said, hugging my mom then patting my dad on the shoulder as I found my seat.

"Did you sleep well last night?" Mom asked.

26

"Oh, yeah, there's nothing like the mountains for a good night's rest. What time are you guys leaving this morning?"

Dad said, "I would like to leave right after breakfast. Is it all right with you?"

"Sure, no problem here."

"We just want to make sure that you and Katie are comfortable and feel safe," Mom added.

"Mom, Dad, this is Mountview. It's just like home, we'll be fine. After all, nothing strange ever happens here."

I really believed that. After all, this was up in the mountains and away from big city crime. In this town, life was just slower.

At that moment, Katie entered the room. "So, what do you think about Austin's dream? Was that weird or what?"

I winced. Katie sat down next to me and whispered, "Well, I guess that makes us even."

She was right. It was annoying, but I had to admire her smooth sneakiness.

"What dream?" my mom asked, looking at me sharply.

I described my dream as simple as possible. I tried to say just enough to satisfy their curiosity. The dream had made a deep impression on me, but I wasn't ready to talk about it much. Besides, I was afraid they would think I was crazy, and I didn't want to worry Mom and Dad when they were about ready to leave.

"You know, Austin," my dad said, "there are people who believe that dreams tell the dreamer about things that are going to happen. These people believe that dreams tell us about the future."

"Really," I said. "Then what do you think my dream means, Dad?"

"Well, let me see," he began, a serious expression on his face. "I think it means that if you don't study, then you will end up sweeping streets for a living."

Mom and Dad got a big laugh out of that.

27

After breakfast, Katie helped Mom clear the table while I helped Dad put their bags in the car. Amy arrived just as we finished.

You know, I think I am onto something. I think that the longer people plan on being away, the longer it takes to say goodbye. Try it sometime. If you are saying goodbye for a day, you just say goodbye. And that's it. If you are saying goodbye for a couple of weeks, then the older people have to give everyone a hug, a longer handshake with about five pumps, and then sometimes another hug. Some of them even think that you have to get a kiss. But when somebody is going away for a month or two, well then there seems to be no end to it. And since my parents were going away, or maybe they were saying that we were going away, whatever, this goodbye was a real long one. There were hugs, and handshakes, and last minute advice, then more hugs, and, of course, the kisses.

When all that was over, I watched as they pulled away. Wow. This was it. I would be here without my mom and dad for the next two months. After what had seemed like an endless wait, my summer adventure had finally begun.

Uncle Steve and Katie went upstairs to do more work on her school project. Amy and I found ourselves alone on the deck, sitting at the table with the big umbrella.

"How do you find someone who doesn't have a phone or a house?" I asked.

"Someone?" Amy asked. "Sarah is a skunk, Austin." She paused for a moment. "OK, she may be a very special skunk, but she is still a skunk. We don't have a phone book for animals." She smiled sympathetically, understanding how troubled I was that we hadn't seen Sarah. "Perhaps Dr. Dixon will have some suggestions. Are you ready to go see him? Steve won't mind if we go without him."

I knew she was right. I suspected that the reason he had made sure Katie was involved in something else was so Amy and I could visit Dr. Dixon without having two extra people tagging along. Uncle Steve was really cool about stuff like that.

Amy and I climbed into her Suburban and drove toward town. The sun was high and the air was warm. Another hour and the sweatshirt would need to go.

Mountview was coming alive as the morning slowly advanced. I saw people walking around. I heard the sound of cars driving by and car doors being slammed, chasing away the morning quiet. Amy suggested taking a walk through town before going to see Dr. Dixon. I jumped at the chance. After all, Mountview had one of the best candy stores in the county.

Amy parked the Suburban at the Old Andrews Inn. We walked along the south sidewalk on Main Street, heading west toward the candy store. As we approached the Mountview Real Estate office, Bill Martin was arranging a display of pictures showing his most recent sales offerings.

Amy said, "Good morning, Bill. Beautiful day, isn't it?"

He looked up and saw Amy and me approaching, "Oh, good morning, Amy. Yes, it's a great day. Hey, and good morning to you, Austin. How are you two doing today?"

"We're just enjoying the day, Bill," Amy replied. "Do you plan to attend the town meeting this Tuesday?"

"It's approaching fast, isn't it? The day after tomorrow will shape the future of our community. I wouldn't miss it for the world," he said while he continued to work on his display.

As soon as we were past Mr. Martin and his office, I looked over at Amy, puzzled.

"How did he know my name?"

Amy shrugged her shoulders. "Just a lucky guess."

As we continued on our way, I took another glance back at Mr. Martin. He noticed me looking and waved. I returned the wave, then walked on, shaking my head.

My steps quickened as we approached a courtyard where several businesses were located. We entered the courtyard and walked up to the third door on the right. This was my favorite place in Mountview. Mr. Bivens had been running the Bivens Candy Store in this spot for as long as I could remember.

When Amy opened the door, we were met by the customary jingling of the bell. "Good morning, Jim," she said.

Mr. Bivens was busy behind the counter. He looked up and smiled. "Good morning, Amy, how are you?" Without giving her a chance to respond, he continued. "And who is this with you?" Once again not giving us the chance to respond, he added, "This must be Austin!"

My eyes shot to meet Amy's eyes. She just smiled.

I looked back at Mr. Bivens, who continued to speak. "It's nice to see you again, Austin. I heard you were coming back for the summer."

Mr. Bivens came around the counter and held out his hand for me to shake. Still in shock, I extended my hand as my parents had taught me.

"It's nice to see you, sir," I said politely. I had been in the store before. I actually had spoken to Mr. Bivens on occasion, but he had never acted this way. I didn't think he even knew my name.

As he shook my hand, Mr. Bivens patted me on the back. "It's not often that we have a local celebrity in my store. Tell you what. This visit is on me. Whatever you would like to pick out today, it's on the house. What do you say?"

I looked at Amy and saw that she was watching me. She smiled and said, "I think Mr. Bivens is waiting for an answer."

"Oh. Yeah," I stammered. "I mean, yes, sir. Thank you very much."

Mr. Bivens said, "Just pick out something. Choose whatever you like." And with that, the bell on the door jingled again and Mr. Bivens turned away to greet his new customer.

Amy walked over to me. "I wanted you to see it for yourself, without me telling you. Pretty cool, isn't it? The townspeople really appreciated you finding the lost children last spring. You left so fast that they didn't have a chance to thank you. But they will, in time."

I was a little embarrassed by this unexpected turn of events, but I had to admit I liked the fact that when we left Mr. Bivens' store I was now in possession of a bag full of colorful jellybeans. The black ones were my favorites. I popped one in my mouth. We left the courtyard shops and continued walking west on the sidewalk along Main Street.

The people we passed on the street offered the customary hellos and good mornings. That was one the great things about Mountview. Everyone was always very friendly.

As we approached the hardware store I saw Mrs. Berry setting up a display on the sidewalk outside the store.

"Good morning, Mrs. Berry, how are you today?" Amy called out.

"Good morning," Mrs. Berry said as she continued to expertly arrange the display. When she turned and saw me, she immediately called out toward the front door of the store, "Harold! Harold, it's that boy, Austin. Harold?"

Harold Berry and his wife Margaret owned and managed Berry's Hardware Store. Mrs. Berry was known for her 'communication efficiency,' as Uncle Steve liked to describe it. 'Right to the point' was her motto, and she was. Most answers were packaged into a simple 'yes' or 'no' – mostly 'no,' I had been told. Uncle Steve always used to say that if you wanted simple, straightforward communication, you should go talk to Margaret Berry.

On the other hand, I had heard that her husband was quite interesting, as conversation goes. Mr. Berry liked to quote people. Perhaps I should change that. Mr. Berry *loved* to quote people. Uncle Steve said Harold Berry had been using quotes for so long that he doubted if Harold knew how to make an original comment. I had been looking forward to meeting this man.

Mr. Berry emerged from his store. "Howdy, folks," he said.

I wondered who had said that before.

Mr. Berry went on. "Hey, Austin, we are very proud of you. I would love to talk to you but I have to get back to work. You know, 'daylight's a burning.'"

I was pretty sure that was a John Wayne line.

Amy said, "Good to see both of you. We won't keep you. We were just walking through town and wanted to say hello."

"Hello, then," said the very efficient Mrs. Berry.

Amy continued, "Do you plan to go to the town meeting?"

I was not surprised when Mrs. Berry merely said, "No."

Mr. Berry said, "I'm going. Absolutely. I have no opinion yet one way or another; I want to wait until we hear more. You know what they say: A handful of patience is worth more than a bushel of brains. I believe that was a Dutch proverb…yes…yes it is, a Dutch proverb."

"Harold," Mrs. Berry said, as if to caution him.

"You know," Mr. Berry continued, "this town meeting will be very important. After all, as Alan Saporta said, 'The best way to escape from a problem is to solve it.'"

"Harold," repeated the economical Mrs. Berry.

Mr. Berry was getting excited now. I could see his eyes begin to twinkle. Despite his wife's interruption, he didn't miss a beat, saying, "'The impossible is often the untried.'" Then he quickly added, "And I believe it was Thomas Edison who said, 'There is no substitute for hard work.' But I think that Bette Davis put it even better when she said, 'Attempt the impossible to improve your work.'"

"Harold!" Mrs. Berry scolded shrilly, her voice echoing down Main Street.

"'It is easier to do a job right than to explain why you didn't,' according to Martin Van Buren." Mr. Berry kept up the pace, as if his 'Play' button was stuck. "We will need to have everyone's opinion and agreement to make this work the right way."

"Harold!" With that last attempt, Mrs. Berry grabbed her husband's sleeve and led him back into the safe confines of their hardware store.

Amy and I watched without saying a word. Mr. Berry's voice faded away as they disappeared into the store.

"Well, that was a nice chat," Amy grinned as we continue along the sidewalk.

After a few steps, we turned and saw Mr. Berry sticking his head out of the hardware store's doorway.

Looking in our direction, he said in a loud whisper, "I agree with Aristotle who said that 'Quality is not an act. It is a habit.' See you Tuesday."

With that, Mr. Berry vanished back into the store, pleased to get in the last word.

We were still laughing about the Berrys when we reached Simms Real Estate. As we walked by, I noticed a drawing of a mountain condo in the office's display window. I stopped and pointed to the picture.

"Amy, is this what Dad was talking about?"

"That's it. What do you think?" she asked.

I stared at the picture. It looked like those big, fancy hotels at Myrtle Beach.

"I think that condo would look great at Myrtle Beach. But not on top of a mountain, especially in Mountview."

Montgomery Simms, the owner of Simms Real Estate, noticed us and opened the door to come outside. He said hello to Amy.

What started as a friendly greeting quickly turned into a discussion of the pros and cons of building the condominium. I listened with increasing interest.

Mr. Simms pointed out the rule of supply and demand. "If enough people want something, then it should be supplied."

Amy agreed, but reminded him that we also needed to protect the environment. "It was here long before we got here and will be here long after we are gone. Therefore, we must respect the environment for what it is. It's not our place to alter it."

A few people heard the conversation and joined us on the sidewalk. One of them was Billy Johnson. Billy worked for *The Mountview Press*, a weekly newspaper that reported on town activities and provided a sounding board for local opinions.

I had overheard Amy and Uncle Steve saying that Billy and the paper had been very busy recently. The hot stories were the chemicals being found in nearby waterways, and the building project. The newspaper had given both subjects a lot of coverage, since everyone in Mountview and the neighboring communities was extremely interested in them. At the moment, interest in the high-rise project was especially keen, since a town council vote on the project was only a few days away.

Billy listened to Amy and Mr. Simms very intently. He was a young reporter who had just recently graduated from the University of Georgia and was interning at the paper for the summer. He knew this was a good story and, like any good reporter, he listened and he took notes.

"Mountview needs a boost," Mr. Simms was saying, "and this project is exactly what will put Mountview on the map."

Amy said, "I agree with you Mr. Simms, but it will put us on the map for the wrong reason."

"How can prosperity be the wrong reason?" Mr. Simms questioned. "Creating space for more people will bring more money, so this town can grow."

"I agree with you that prosperity and growth are good." Amy understood Mr. Simms' point, but he wasn't getting her point. She tried again. "But we need planned growth, controlled growth that protects the environment. That is far more important for long-term prosperity."

As the discussion continued, more people stopped to listen. A crowd was gathering. One person attracted to this crowd was approaching from the west. Just by watching him, I could see that he liked being the center of attention. Here was a crowd, and he was not about to miss the chance. I watched him as he studied the group. *Ah, there is a reporter; how nice,* I imagined he was thinking.

The man skillfully maneuvered through the crowd until he was face to face with Amy and Mr. Simms. He was tall, probably about six foot three or six foot four. His slender frame, coupled with his above average height and unusually pale skin, made him appear to be thinner than he actually was. At a distance, he had appeared to be in his mid 40's. As he approached, he looked older. Despite the appearance of wealth, which often keeps people protected from daily worries, this man must have had worries of another kind. His eyes were dark and sunken, with an almost frightening appearance, as though they had witnessed something tragic. His hair was a little too long. Brushed back from his forehead, it appeared slightly wet or greasy. The closer he came, the older he looked.

The man listened, patiently waiting for his chance to be heard. What I would find out later was this was how he always operated. He used the power of his size and his words to manipulate. When necessary, he didn't hesitate to use the power of his name and his money to be sure that he would get his way. But his weapons of choice had always been his voice and his words. He knew that his voice had the power to captivate. It was a deep voice, spiced with fancy words delivered like he was some sort of preacher. He appeared to be an educated, cultured man. The honeyed tones of his voice conveyed wisdom, compassion, and caring for the well-being of others. Like so many things in life, appearances were deceiving.

"Excuse me," he said, speaking slowly in his deep, rich voice. "I am DeWitt Pickett. I happen to be a developer and owner of a rather large parcel of land here in Mountview. I could not help but overhear your remarks."

As the words rolled out of his mouth, he spoke each syllable clearly, almost as if he were singing. I had never met this man before, but I did not like him. Mom had always told me not to form opinions quickly, but I sensed something - something that felt wrong, or even evil.

Mr. Pickett nodded politely toward Amy. "You are absolutely correct, young lady. It is critical for any development in this community to be studied and controlled." He smiled and looked around at the crowd, as if to draw them closer to him. "Believe me, I know that well. I am on the board of the group proposing the building project. We have spent countless hours reviewing the plans to ensure that our beloved community will not be harmed."

Amy watched what he was doing, getting the crowd to agree with him. She said, "Then how could you choose to build in an area like Sunset Rock? That is a beautiful natural setting. It's a historical treasure for this area. Your building project will alter its natural state forever."

Without missing a beat, Mr. Pickett calmly responded. "Exactly. We will preserve our treasured land by erecting a monument to our past that will allow many, not just a few, to witness what nature has bestowed upon us. Development will come to Mountview. That is certain. If it isn't today, it will be tomorrow. Perhaps it will not happen until after we are gone, and then when it does, we won't be here to control it. Now is the time for us to build. Now, before outsiders build. We will develop Mountview our way, the right way, and preserve nature."

The crowd seemed to agree with that. I could see it, and so could Amy. She spoke again. Her voice was quiet, but you could see in her face how strongly she felt about what she was saying.

"You don't protect nature by altering it or by building upon it. You protect nature by preserving it. I say the town should buy the land and make it into a park where everyone can enjoy it. Just like you said, Mr. Pickett, to allow many, not just a few, to witness what nature has bestowed upon us."

Several people nodded in agreement. Billy Johnson was listening intently and probably praying - praying that the batteries in his little Sony tape recorder would hold out so he would not miss a moment of this discussion. He pushed the little recorder closer to the action.

I sensed that Mr. Pickett could feel the discussion slipping away. I bet that he hadn't expected Amy to be such a difficult adversary. I could feel him wanting to back away gracefully and do battle another day. Later, I would find out that the right battleground for him would be the town meeting. He knew how to stir up a crowd, and he would come prepared. He knew the town was still behind him at this moment; he didn't want to lose their vote or the momentum. Tuesday night he would put the final nail in the coffin. All he needed was to get to Tuesday night without problems.

He scanned the audience and decided to act as the Southern gentleman that his father had hoped in vain that he would be. "Ladies and gentlemen, there seem to be two sides here, as with any issue; those for it and those against it. I will honor the words of my esteemed fellow citizen and ask that we all adjourn this discussion until Tuesday night at the Town Council meeting. As my dear father used to say, 'Respect the opinions of others, so that they will respect yours.'"

Mr. Pickett looked around at this audience and that's when he noticed me staring him. He returned my stare for a long moment, as if to say, *'Good, this is a great way for me to win the crowd before I leave. Always involve the children; people love it because it builds your case with compassion.'*

"Hello, young man," he said, looking at me but actually speaking to the crowd. "Here is someone from Mountview's next generation. Let's ask his opinion. So, young man, what do you think about having a beautiful, tall new building right here in Mountview?"

I didn't have to think. I knew exactly what to say. "Mr. Pickett, I believe that chopping off the top of a beautiful mountain would be like taking a beautiful girl and giving her a flat top."

The crowd roared with laughter.

I continued, "Yes, sir, I *am* the next generation, and I would be forced to look at that flat top for the rest of my life. I vote no."

Mr. Pickett took a deep breath. The crowd was still laughing. Billy Johnson was checking his batteries and a smile of relief filled his face. *Yes, the tape was still going; got the whole thing.*

Mr. Pickett realized he had lost this battle. He did the only thing a person in his position could do. He laughed. Then he patted me on the head and said, "Oh, kids will be kids." He smiled indulgently as if I was cute, but not too bright. "Ladies and gentlemen, I have to go. Thanks, everyone." With that, he walked away.

Mr. Pickett turned to look back at the crowd as he crossed the street. His deep, penetrating stare was like a heat-seeking missile trying to find its target. I peeked around the protective cover of the group and unexpectedly found that I was the target of this new-found enemy. *I will get you,* Mr. Pickett's gaze clearly communicated. I understood the message.

A cold chill suddenly came over me and I realized I was frightened of this man. I was a young boy, without my parents here to protect me. I would have to defend myself.

Chapter 5

The crowd began to disperse. Billy Johnson was the last to leave. "You don't mind if I quote you, do you?" Billy asked me.

"No, I don't mind. What exactly are you going to quote me saying?" I wondered.

"Oh, probably a little of what you said about the town; something about the building. You know, nothing much. Hey, I have to go. See you later," Billy told me and trotted off.

Amy and I crossed the street and headed back to the car.

"You were pretty cool back there, Amy."

"I wasn't the one that everybody liked, Austin. You were a big hit." And with that, she patted me on the shoulder. As we approached the car, she added "It's time to go see Dr. Dixon."

She started the Suburban and drove across town. Within a few minutes she pulled up to the Dixons' house. We walked up to the door and rang the bell. We waited for a minute, then Mrs. Dixon opened the door.

"Hello, Mrs. Dixon, how are you today?" Amy asked.

"Well, if it isn't Amy Bryant. Hello, dear, it's so nice to see you. And look here," she said looking at me. "Another good friend has come to see us. It's nice to see you, too, Austin."

Mrs. Dixon was wonderful. Her smile reminded me of Amy's. Perhaps years ago she might have even looked like Amy. The years had been kind to Mrs. Dixon. And that was only fair. Mrs. Dixon was kind to everyone.

"Hello, Mrs. Dixon. It is nice to see you, too."

"You must come in. Reeves will be thrilled that you came to visit us." And with that, we entered. She closed the door behind us and ushered us into the living room.

Dr. Dixon came into the room. "Two of my favorite people! How lucky I am today. Hello, Amy. Hello, Austin."

"Hello, Dr. Dixon," we both replied.

Amy began, "The town is buzzing with discussion about the high-rise."

"Yes it is. You'd think Mountview never had a high-rise before," Dr. Dixon joked. "What's all the fuss about anyway?"

"I don't think it is such a laughing matter." Mrs. Dixon said. "The Town Council is split fifty - fifty on this issue. Tuesday's town meeting will be a humdinger. You know our vote will be taken the next day. This vote will shape our community forever. It really is exciting; I can't wait."

"We ran into Mr. Pickett today. He was his usual pleasant self," Amy said sarcastically.

"Be careful, Amy," Mrs. Dixon warned. "DeWitt Pickett is not just unpleasant. He can be downright mean!"

"Austin sure made an impression on him today, didn't you, Austin?" Amy prompted.

I hadn't stopped thinking about it. The way he had looked when he left. The threatening message that his eyes sent. "Yes, I might have said something that didn't sit well with him."

"Well, it wasn't so bad that Austin said something, but Billy Johnson was there, recording every word," Amy said.

"Then tomorrow's paper should be quite interesting. What did you say to him, Austin?" Dr. Dixon asked.

I repeated what I had said. The Dixons thought it was funny. When I mentioned that the idea came to me because of a dream, it occurred to me that Dr. Dixon was all about dreams. He would not let that statement go without more questions.

I wasn't surprised when he said, "Why don't we go to my office and talk a little bit more about this dream of yours?"

Amy, Dr. Dixon, and I walked into the study. I liked this warm, comfortable room, with its dark, leather furniture, bookshelves loaded with all kinds of books, and the two large windows that allowed sunlight and fresh air to pour into the room. We each pulled up a chair into the middle of the room and sat down.

"So, what about this dream, Austin? By the way, did you ever go see any of my associates regarding your telepathic powers?"

"No, sir. It seemed a little too strange," I admitted. "And after a while, it just didn't seem to matter. But I received your letter, and have it right here in my pocket."

"OK, I understand, and it's good that you kept the letter. I've been looking forward to this summer, since you will be staying here for so long. Perhaps we will learn more about these powers. But for now, let's hear about your dream."

"Yes, sir." I remembered the dream and told him in as much detail as I could remember. Dr. Dixon listened intently, waiting patiently until I was finished. He removed his glasses and tilted his head upward, closing his eyes. It was as if he was imagining something as he replayed my words.

"So this Indian princess had a turquoise necklace." He paused. "And the necklace was very unique; in the shape of an animal, but an animal that you had never seen. The light seemed to be emanating, or I mean coming from it, you say. Hmmm. So, how did you feel about this princess?"

I thought about that. How did I feel about the princess? Feel? It was just a dream. I really didn't know what he meant. Finally, I said, "I'm not sure I understand your question."

"Did you feel comfortable, scared, worried, in love?" Dr. Dixon asked innocently.

I laughed. What did he mean, in love? Was he kidding? "Well, I guess I felt a little frightened, but not scared. I knew I wasn't in danger. Is that what you mean?"

"Yes, that is exactly what I mean. Now, tell me more. Please describe everything you can remember about this princess, and especially about the necklace."

Well, I'll give it a try, I thought as I sat on the edge of the chair. "The princess had long, dark hair. She wore a brown dress that reminded me of a deerskin that was tanned, made for wearing. She had a bracelet - I noticed that when she first sat up. Her face was darker than mine and she had an even darker spot near one eye. I've seen that once before; Mom says they're called beauty marks. She had a necklace around her neck." There was something hanging from the necklace that I wanted to remember. What was it? Oh, yeah. "The necklace had a large silver chain, but there was a piece of turquoise – it was big, too – hanging from the silver chain, and it was definitely in the shape of an animal. I couldn't tell what kind of animal it was. The reason I remember it so well is because the turquoise animal was glowing."

I made a gesture with my hands to show what I meant. Dr. Dixon seemed to be more interested in the princess and the necklace than he was in the dream itself. Maybe that was how dreams were interpreted. I didn't know.

"I must say you either have a very vivid imagination or a very good memory of this person. Perhaps you saw a picture at one time, and now that image came to mind? Could you have seen a picture of her at your Uncle's house?"

"Yes, sir, I have been told that I have quite an imagination. But I don't believe I have ever seen a picture of her before, and definitely not a picture of the necklace. Why?"

"Well, Austin, there is no mistaking that necklace. What you described is clearly a necklace with a history. It is, or should I say was, quite unique. I may have a picture of it. Let's see here."

Dr. Dixon turned and began searching for a book on his bookcase. He looked over the books in the upper shelf, then he turned his attention to the shelf just below it. I glanced over at Amy who looked at me and raised her eyebrows as if to say, 'He seems to be onto something.' I looked back at

Dr. Dixon just as he pulled a book from the shelf and began to leaf through it. Clearly, he was looking for something specific.

As he scanned the pages, he continued. "This necklace was believed to have some kind of power. Some magical power, if my memory serves me right. The necklace was well documented largely due to its unique substances." Dr. Dixon looked up from the book and spoke directly to us. "See, turquoise is not a native stone to this area. So where did it come from? No one knows and I have never been able to find out. Now, there were discoveries of silver and gold in this area, but the Native Indians at this time and in this part of the country didn't use silver. So where did the silver come from? No one knows that either. So it is easy to understand why such a necklace was easy to trace." Dr. Dixon turned his attention back to his book. His finger was turning pages. "Now, if my memory serves me right...oh yes, here it is." He stared at the picture for moment, lost in thought. Then he looked up at Amy and me and continued speaking, as if he hadn't interrupted himself. "And then the necklace simply vanished. No one knows what happened to it. It just disappeared from existence."

Dr. Dixon turned the book towards me and Amy so that we could get a better look.

"Austin, is this the necklace and the turquoise animal that you saw?"

Amy and I studied the picture.

"Wow! That's the necklace, all right. It's beautiful. But the color was much more, you know..." I was gesturing, trying to find the word.

"Radiant?" asked Dr. Dixon.

"Yes, sir, that is exactly it, radiant. It seemed to glow."

Amy commented, "It really is quite beautiful. What kind of animal is that, Dr. Dixon?"

Dr. Dixon paused for a moment, as if collecting his thoughts. Amy and I stared at him intently. He cleared his throat.

"Allow me to enlighten you. Austin Cook, Amy Bryant, meet T'shoo Imone Ennee... also known as The Schmooney!"

There was silence in the room.

Then I raised my fist into the air and shouted, "Yes!" That seemed to break the spell.

"So there really is a Schmooney," Amy said. It wasn't a question. It was more like she was restating a fact, in order to make sure she had understood.

"Yes, there is, Amy," Dr. Dixon answered quietly, "and it appears it is time for us to share what we know."

I looked at the picture again. On the opposite side of the page, there were more pictures. There was a picture of an Indian teepee, a picture of an Indian on a horse, and then there was a picture of someone wearing the turquoise necklace. I hadn't noticed it before. As I studied the person in the picture, I became even more excited.

"Dr. Dixon, not only is that the necklace, but this is the girl!" I exclaimed, pointing to the picture.

Dr. Dixon turned the book around and studied the picture. Then he looked at me.

"Are you certain? Are you sure that's who visited you in your dream?"

"Yes, sir, definitely; that was the princess. See the beauty mark beneath her left eye? I remember that."

Dr. Dixon looked at the picture again, then stared at me, sizing up the situation. He turned his attention back to the picture and said, "I should know better by now, but you continue to amaze me."

He put the book down and said, "So, Austin, you not only talk to skunks these days, but you also have a three hundred-year-old princess visiting you in the night? There never seems to be a dull moment with you, young man."

He sat back down in his chair. There was silence for a moment.

Then Amy said slowly, "Did I hear you correctly, a three hundred-year-old princess?" She shook her head in disbelief.

Dr. Dixon was cleaning his glasses. "Yes, you understood me correctly. It appears that a three hundred-year-old princess has visited our intriguing young man here."

I looked at Amy and Dr. Dixon and said, "Cool."

"Yes, very cool indeed. Make no mistake about it; Princess Onnat Minti visited you, Austin. She was a descendant of the Choctaw Nation and the Chickasaw Indian tribe that settled in the Carolinas and lived right around this area in the 1700's. I'm sure you recognize her name, from the lake that carries that name to this day. But what makes this story most interesting is something else.

"Legend has it that her father, Chief Kostini Hatak, had a vision that his beautiful daughter was destined for greatness, but that her destiny would only be achieved with the help of a Schmooney. Her unusual necklace was made to honor the Schmooney, and to serve as a constant reminder of her destiny. To help ensure her success, the Chief offered his daughter in marriage to any brave who could prove that a Schmooney existed. Sadly, none could. The princess died a very lonely woman, bound by the solitude that could be ended only by a Schmooney. It is said that her ghost still walks the land looking for the brave who can deliver her father's wish and release her from her earthly exile."

"Wow!" I was silent for a moment, letting all of that sink in. "So why did she say, 'Austin, we need your help. Help us, please?' What am I supposed to do?"

"Now *that* is the big question. Apparently, you are in a position to help her. You just don't know it. On the other hand…."

Dr. Dixon's voice faded away. He stopped looking at me and looked toward the floor, in very deep thought.

Amy looked at me questioningly. I shrugged. Amy looked back at Dr. Dixon.

"Excuse me, Dr. Dixon, what seems to be the matter?"

He didn't seem to hear the question.

So Amy said louder, "Dr. Dixon? Dr. Dixon?"

Startled, he looked up. "Oh, I'm sorry. Yes?"

"You said, 'on the other hand…,'" Amy reminded him. "What did you mean?"

"Oh, yes. Well, I was just thinking that perhaps her message was about not the past, but the future. Yes…something may be about to happen. She knows it, but we don't."

He looked directly into my eyes and spoke slowly and clearly. "Austin, you need to prepare yourself."

I didn't know what to say to that.

Dr. Dixon nodded, understanding my confusion. "Now, let me tell you what I know about the Schmooney." He settled back comfortably in his chair. "Why don't I begin by telling you what little I know about this ancient creature that still roams our forests today?

"There have been many stories written and passed down over generations about animals that roam the earth protecting other animals. There are ancient writings from cultures in many different parts of the world that portray a supreme animal that protects all the creatures on the earth. And American Indian folklore describes a creature that roams the night, always on the alert, ready to help animals recognize and flee danger."

"So the story that Uncle Steve read, 'The Legend of the Schmooney,' is true?" I asked.

"Yes, Austin, it could be very true." Dr. Dixon looked at me apologetically. "I'm sorry I had to make you think that I didn't believe it when we talked before. But I have to discredit that story when people ask me about it. I can't let people know the legend is true. They would start running around capturing animals, trying to find one that speaks. Can you imagine that happening? It would be bad for the animals and bad for the people. Or imagine someone trying to have a conversation with a bear. That would be suicide."

"Yes, sir, that would be crazy," I agreed. "Tell us more. When did you first hear about a Schmooney?"

"The first time was many years ago. I was working for the State of North Carolina Bureau of Natural Resources. I was looking for some historical detail – gosh, I don't even remember what I was looking for. It's been so many years – I was reading some of Daniel Boone's diary to see if I could find what I needed. The diary mentioned an Indian legend about a 'protector of the forest.' That was the first time that I saw the name,

T'shoo Imone Ennee. So the legend existed before Daniel Boone's time. The Indians in Western Carolina knew the legend, but I've never found any written reports earlier than that diary entry by Daniel Boone."

"But what about the necklace and Princess Onnat Minti?" I prompted him.

"The necklace? Ah yes, the necklace. It seems that the Princess's daddy, Chief Kostini Hatak, had heard about the legend, too. He had always wanted to know if the legend was real or not. Then, after he had the vision about the Schmooney's part in his daughter's destiny, finding a Schmooney became an obsession. He challenged all of his braves to find a Schmooney and prove that the legend was real. He offered his daughter's hand in marriage to any brave who could do that.

"The Chief had his most skilled craftsman make a turquoise necklace that was so beautiful it was often described as radiant. It was said that the image of the Schmooney glowed like a beacon, as if it were calling to the Schmooney. His daughter wore the necklace always, symbolizing that the Schmooney's presence would dictate her life.

"Unfortunately, as Indian folklore shows, the Chief never saw a Schmooney and his daughter died a very lonely woman. But death did not release her from the curse that her father's vision turned out to be. She still walks the earth looking for a real Schmooney. When she finds it and her destiny is fulfilled, the curse will be lifted, the turquoise necklace will lose its magical power, and she will finally depart this world and move on to a place of eternal peace."

"Why was it so hard to find a Schmooney?" I asked.

"You might be able to find one, my dear Austin, because you have a special power. Very few people have the power to find a Schmooney. I explained that to you in my letter. At the time of the Indian legend, no one had that power. Does that help you understand the enormity of this incredible gift that you have? Do you understand the power that you yield?"

"Yes, sir, I think so. I am trying to understand all of this, but it is not easy. What kind of power does the Schmooney have? What does it take to find one? And what about the power of the necklace?"

"The power of the Schmooney. That was the irony of the whole situation. The Schmooney was almost certainly there; it may have always been there. But no one could sense it. No one knew it. You see, the Schmooney has the power to be any animal that it wants to be. Think about that. It can change into any animal. That's precisely why we never see it; because we always see it, we just don't realize it. It takes a very special person to recognize it, to communicate with it. You, Austin, have that ability."

I spoke softly, thinking out loud. "So if a Schmooney can change into another animal, and that animal then would have the Schmooney's power to communicate, or to telepathically communicate…and since Sarah, who is a skunk – at least we think that's what she is – has the power to communicate with me…."

I looked up at Dr. Dixon. "Then, is Sarah a Schmooney?"

"Yes, Austin. That is exactly what Sarah is. Sarah is a Schmooney."

"So that is why Sarah sent me the message, 'Don't be alarmed, but the next time you see me, I may look totally different.'"

"Yes, that's right. She can change into any other animal - a bird, or maybe even a human. I really don't know what the whole power of the Schmooney may be. But if the legend is correct, a Schmooney is here to help the other animals. I'm very glad that she is on our team."

"How does she change into another animal? You know, how does that work?"

"Well, I don't really know, Austin. I became very interested and spent a great deal of my free time searching for answers. I read so many old manuscripts that I developed a reputation for being the regional expert on Indian folklore. That was a good thing. I went for long walks in the forest, just hoping that a Schmooney would jump out and say, 'Here I am, Doc, what do you think?' I was going crazy. Fortunately, I met a wonderful woman. She understood dedication. She understood that I was in search of answers. And she understood me. We fell in love. And that woman became Mrs. Reeves Dixon."

"She is a lovely woman," Amy said, smiling. "But tell me, why did Sarah tell Austin that you knew her?"

"Oh, yes. Well, one day when I was walking through the forest, I came upon an injured owl. I bundled her up and took her to Western Carolina University. That was before we had Amy or the Nature Museum in Mountview. The folks at WCU were wonderful. They nursed the owl back to health and released her within a year. Shortly afterward, an owl visited me. I knew it wasn't the same one, because the owl we released had distinctive markings. This owl was quite brave. She literally sat in a tree right next to our back porch and called. She called to me every evening. We became friends. She would visit and I would sit on the porch. I started talking to her, and sometimes I even imagined that she understood what I was saying."

"Did she have a name? What did you call her?" I asked.

"Yes, I gave her a name. I named her Sarah."

Chapter 6

Amy and I drove back to Uncle Steve's house. How quickly the time had passed. It had been a wild day, learning so much about the people in Mountview and about the history in this area. I learned a whole lot of stuff that I would need to think about.

Amy and I could not stop thinking about Sarah. I wanted to take another walk and look for her, but it was getting late in the day and everyone was resting.

Dinner came and went, with Amy cooking chicken on the grill and Uncle Steve cleaning up afterwards. Yes, you heard me right, Uncle Steve cleaned up afterwards. Apparently, he had lost a bet to Katie. It had something to do with the school project and Katie had won.

Since Katie and I didn't have dishes to do, we decided to go to Uncle Steve's office and look through books. I wanted to read more of *The Count of Monte Cristo* so I stopped in the library for the book and met Katie upstairs in the office.

Katie immediately went for pictures. There was a large picture book called *The Natural Beauty of North Carolina*. It was a favorite of Katie's because it was filled with pictures of sunrises, sunsets, mountains, rivers and animals that live in the state. She found it and spread it open on the floor to look at the pictures. I sank into a comfortable chair and started to read.

I was absorbed in my book, reading about how Dantes was getting his revenge, when Katie said, "Remember those pictures of Uncle Steve and the Army people?"

I looked up from my book. "What did you say?"

"You know, Uncle Steve and the Army guys? Where are those pictures?"

"I don't know," I told her as I looked over toward the bookshelves and scanned a few shelves. "Why do you want to see them?"

"Well," she pointed to a picture, "there's a picture here of a big bear, like the one we saw in those pictures."

"That picture of the bear is downstairs in the library," I said, correcting her.

"No it isn't. It's in the pictures we saw in the book," Katie said defiantly.

"No, it isn't." I knew I was right, but why argue. "But who cares."

"I know it's there. You're wrong," Katie insisted.

I sighed and said, "OK, let's find out who's right." I put my book down and went over to the shelves. I looked in several places, and finally pulled out a gray scrapbook from underneath a pile of books. Katie crawled over next to me. We sat cross-legged on the floor with the book in front of us. Since it looked a bit ragged, we opened it carefully, to make certain nothing fell out or fell apart.

There we saw the pictures I had flipped through once before. Plastic covers protected some of the pictures. There were pictures of Dad with sideburns and a couple with Uncle Steve in a beard. We both agreed the beard looked fake. When we turned to the next page, one whole side was filled with pictures of people in camouflage clothes and guns. In another picture Uncle Steve was kneeling next to an animal that was dead. We kept turning pages. This was a photo album, a collection of Uncle Steve's memories. Then we got to the Army guys.

"They have guns. Hey, look, this is Uncle Steve." I pointed to our uncle standing in the middle of three other Army guys. In the other pictures, the ones toward the front of the book, Uncle Steve had been smiling. But in this one, and then the next, and the next, he wasn't smiling.

"Look, he isn't smiling in this picture or that picture, or in any of these pictures," I said, and we looked more closely at each picture.

50

Then a voice from the doorway said, "No, I wasn't smiling."

Katie screamed. I was startled, too. I jerked my head around to look toward the door, but I managed not to scream.

It was Uncle Steve, of course.

"Sorry, didn't mean to scare you," he said, coming over to sit with us. "I didn't have much to smile about back then. That was a long time ago. Why don't we close the book and get ready for tomorrow? It should be a big day."

"Why didn't you smile?" Katie asked.

"Well, let's just say I was in the Army, doing Army things. The Army is very serious business. So I was very serious." Uncle Steve sat on the floor next to Katie, stroking her hair. He wasn't really looking at either of us. He continued, almost as if he was talking to himself. "Things were very different back then."

He stopped talking, and just kept his hand resting lightly on top of Katie's head. He held it there for a few moments, just staring – just staring at nothing.

Suddenly, he opened his eyes wide and said, "Well, here I am. I'm back. What's on the agenda for tomorrow?"

"We're going out for breakfast," Katie said firmly.

"And then we get to go to the Nature Museum," I said.

"OK. I'll drop you guys off at the Museum and then meet up with you and Amy here tomorrow night. OK? That's the plan. What time shall I set the alarm, to wake us for breakfast?"

"I don't need an alarm clock," I told him. "I can get up wherever I want to. It's like I have this internal clock."

"Oh, I've heard about those internal clocks," said Uncle Steve. "That is very handy to have. So what you are saying is that you can get all of us up and I shouldn't worry about setting the alarm?"

"Yep, I'll be up waiting for you, just wait and see. Oh, Uncle Steve, where is the picture of you and that big black bear?" I asked, wanting to get that matter cleared up. After all, I knew I was right.

"That picture is in the library. Why?"

"No reason, I just was wondering," I said innocently as I made a face at Katie. "Just wondering."

This time not only did Katy stick her tongue out, but she also crossed her eyes. I was impressed. I didn't know she could cross her eyes; another discovery. The last couple of days had been one surprise after another and one discovery after another. I wondered how many more discoveries were out there.

* * * * *

It was about this time that another discovery was taking place that I wasn't aware of at that time. I'll tell you what was taking place.

The sun rising over one of the most beautiful lakes in the area is an amazing sight. Lake Minti was awakening to another new day, with the birds chirping happily and the waters bubbling with new fish life. The forest animals were making the morning trek to their favorite water source. It was just another normal day in the life of that critical link in the ecosystem.

If you listened very carefully, you could hear the gentle gurgling of the water in Jackson's Stream as it cascaded over rocks into the lake before emptying the precious liquid it had gathered over the many miles of the Sunset Plateau. If you looked very carefully at Jackson's Stream, peering through the large and small pines that guarded the entrance, and if you peeled back all the brush that covered that area, you would see not only the welcome water trickling over the rocks, but you might also see something not so welcome. Unfortunately, no one had detected it. Yet.

Mercury is a naturally occurring metal and the primary source of contaminations from the burning of fossil fuels. Rain wipes mercury from emissions of coal burning power furnaces, washing it into our water sources. There, bacteria transform mercury to an organic form called methyl mercury, which works its way up the food chain to fish.

"When most citizens hear 'mercury', they think of the silver stuff in thermometers," Harvey Gaines had recently been quoted in the *Mountview Press*. "That's common stuff, but it's not the same as what we get in fish. The mercury in fish gets into the people who eat the fish, ending mercury's trip to the top of the food chain."

In humans, mercury attacks the nervous system, creating vision and memory problems and a bunch of other bad things. Heavy metals such as mercury and lead build-up in the body over time, making them very difficult to get rid of. Infants and children are particularly sensitive to the effects of mercury since their nervous systems are still forming.

The health effects of high levels of mercury were well known to one new resident of Mountview, Frances Evans. She had a very good idea where her mercury poisoning came from, and she knew it was *not* from Mountview. Frances had moved her family to Mountview because of the clean, crisp air and the naturally clean water. She wanted to give her family the chance she had never had. But having lived in a contaminated industrial area for many years, she would never forget what mercury had done to her. "I thought I was dying," she had said when Billy Johnson interviewed her. "I had lived in that area my entire life and had eaten a lot of fish from the streams and rivers around there, not thinking anything about it."

Mercury had suppressed her immune system, making her susceptible to a variety of medical problems. She was in Mountview because she wanted to get away from those problems. Unfortunately, those problems had found Frances Evans once again. But what made it even more threatening this time was that those problems would also find the family she was trying to protect.

As Mr. Gaines had told the reporter, "Although mercury levels are increasing, it's still safe to eat many fish. Rainbow trout, brown trout, small mouth bass, redbreast sunfish and bluegill are OK. But largemouth and spotted bass should not be eaten more than once a week."

Harvey Gaines had always bragged about how clean Lake Minti was. He wanted to be able to continue to brag about the lake. He was determined that he would find and correct the problem. He would bet his life on it. The members of Frances Evans' family were betting their lives on him, too. They just didn't know it.

Chapter 7

The morning started early for me. The sun wasn't shining in its customary fashion. Actually, the sun wasn't to be found at all. Since there were very few clocks at Uncle Steve's, I didn't know what time it was. I looked over at Katie, who was still asleep. I figured it must be early, so I rolled over and shut my eyes.

I was dreaming. I was floating on a cloud, somewhere high over the Appalachian Mountains. I could see for miles and miles. It was beautiful. The wind was gentle against my face. I was gaining speed. I was going faster and faster. At first this had been fun. Now, it was getting too fast for me. I was being pushed up and down and up and down. The turbulence was rough - too rough. I was getting sick from all the pushing. I had to do something; I was losing control. I was heading straight for a big, bright light, squinting to try to see how to avoid hitting it. *Stop, stop!* I thought desperately.

Suddenly my eyes opened wide and I saw Uncle Steve. His hands were on my shoulders, rolling me around.

"Time to get up, Austin. Get up, Austin."

"OK, OK, I'm up. Stop shaking me. I'm going to puke."

"Come on, Big Ben, your internal clock must have stopped." Uncle Steve grinned.

I heard Katie laughing, "I thought you were the guy that could get up without an alarm."

I put a pillow over my head. "I was up hours ago."

"Oh, sure you were. I get the bathroom first," Katie announced, and a moment later she was closing the bathroom door behind her.

"I'll be downstairs, ready to go whenever you guys are ready." And with that, Uncle Steve headed down the stairs.

I lay in bed, thinking of my stomach and saying over and over again to myself *I won't puke. I won't puke.* As my stomach began to settle, my thoughts drifted off to other things. I thought about my mom and dad. I wasn't homesick, but I did miss them. I thought about Sarah and wondered if I would see her again. My thoughts drifted to flying over the mountains. I could see forever. I was soaring, soaring above the clouds, and then all of a sudden, BOOM! What an explosion. It was like a lightning bolt!

A message hit me. It was Sarah. Sarah! I could feel her presence as if she were right next to me. She was yelling, *'I need your help. Come as quickly as you can!'*

My eyes opened wide. I shot up in bed and instinctively answered, "I will. I'll help!"

I tried to send her a message but nothing happened. It was as if someone had hung up the phone. The connection was lost. I tried again, but no luck. I wasn't feeling very well to begin with, after all that flying and diving, but this made me wonder. I figured I just needed some food and some solid ground to stand on for awhile, and then I would know what to do.

Uncle Steve was waiting on the back deck with Katie when I came outside. He was looking up at the sky and saying, "Looks like it could get a little wet today." Then he saw me. "Well, here he is. You don't look so good, Austin. Are you all right?"

"Mmmmm," I said, nodding my head.

"You'll feel better after you get some food. You need something more in your stomach than just an internal clock." Then he laughed.

"Very funny," I said glaring at Katie who was giggling at Uncle Steve's joke.

It was cloudy and dark outside. It was only 7:30 in the morning, so there were still long shadows from the tall trees around us. We got into the Jeep and headed into town.

One of our favorite breakfast spots was the Open Hearth. Uncle Steve was a regular and everyone there was always very nice. The food was good and they served grits.

We walked in and several people greeted us. Some of them said hello to me, calling me by name, which was really cool. I waved and said good morning.

One elderly man who was just leaving said, "Who cares what kids think?"

None of us knew what he meant by that. We sat down. The waitress came over and we ordered breakfast. When she was picking up the menus she said, "I think you're right on the money, Austin." She walked away before I could ask her what she meant.

We looked at each other, confused. Uncle Steve got a copy of the *Mountview Press* and began to read the local news section.

The Open Hearth has crayons and paper for kids to draw with while they wait for their food. Katie started drawing something. I think it was an animal or maybe a car, it was hard to tell. Uncle Steve was reading the local paper, and I was looking at the other people in the restaurant.

It was fun to people watch. There was a game I liked to play, where I looked at people (trying not to stare) and I imagined what they did for a living. Then I tried to guess what kind of car they drove and what they had ordered to eat. It was fun. I was right more times than I was wrong, about the food they had ordered. I never had the chance to check out any of my other guesses.

I scanned the restaurant and noticed a couple sitting by the front window. They were older, probably 50 or so. He had lines on his face so I figured he probably worked outside. He was a pleasant-looking fellow; he looked like he might be somebody's grandfather. He was wearing those dark blue farmer overalls; I think they call them bib overalls. They're one piece with straps that go over the shoulders and clip to the main part. They were faded, but clean. He had a baseball cap on with 'John Deere' written on it along with a picture of a green deer. I have seen those before.

The woman across from him, whose back was to me, was wearing a white sweater that probably buttoned down the front. She had gray hair and no hat, but I couldn't see her face.

I decided that he was a farmer and she was his wife. I guessed that he drove an old Ford pickup truck, probably blue. As far as breakfast; he would want eggs, over easy, and bacon and toast. He was already drinking coffee. She would get the same. That was my guess. They weren't reading a newspaper, like Uncle Steve and like most everybody else in the restaurant was. They weren't talking to each other either. They were just kind of sitting there, looking out the window between sips of coffee. The waitress walked up to the table with their food. Her back was facing me so I couldn't see what she brought them. I moved my head to try to see around her, but couldn't so I waited for her to leave. I could see his plate - eggs, bacon, and toast. Yes! Was I good or what? I saw his wife's breakfast - eggs, toast, and no meat. Oh well, five out of six wasn't bad.

I looked at a couple of other tables; mostly families, nobody really interesting. My eyes wandered to the back of the restaurant where I noticed a man sitting by himself. He was wearing a dirty, red flannel shirt that looked like he had slept in it. His jeans were worn and he had boots on that needed some polish. His baseball cap was on the table and his hair was all messed up. I guessed that he probably slept someplace that I didn't want to know about and decided that I didn't want to know what he ordered, either. So I stopped the game.

I heard Uncle Steve rustling the paper. I glanced over and saw that he was looking at me over the top of it. Just staring. He had been holding the paper up in front of his face while he read, so his eyebrows, eyes and part of his nose were all that was visible. He held that position for several moments.

"What?" I asked defensively.

"Well, look what we have here," he said. Katie looked up from her drawing.

Uncle Steve folded the paper and turned it around so we could see it. There it was, a picture of Amy and me taken yesterday when we were in town talking to that group of people. There was an article titled, "Local Hero Speaks Out About High Rise." As if that wasn't enough, I got an even bigger surprise. Next to our picture was a drawing of a beautiful woman with long hair, and the top of her hair was cut in a flat top. The words below the picture said, "Come to Mountview; it could be a hair-raising experience."

Katie started laughing. "What's wrong with her hair?" she asked.

My mouth was hanging open. I was shocked. Uncle Steve read the article to us.

> Mountview Building Project discussions reached a new height yesterday when local hero, twelve-year-old Austin Cook, shared his feelings with Mountview residents.
>
> Ms. Amy Bryant, Park Ranger and Director of Mountview Nature Museum, and Mr. Montgomery Simms, owner of Simms Real Estate, engaged in a friendly discussion of the proposed project on Main Street outside Mr. Simms' office.
>
> Mr. Simms expressed the benefits of the new condominium, pointing out that it would provide our community with a project that would fuel growth and prosperity. Ms. Bryant supports growth and prosperity, but she voiced concerns that uncontrolled development could destroy the natural settings that make Mountview such a beautiful place.
>
> This constructive discussion attracted the attention of several other residents, which then unexpectedly turned humorous when Mr. DeWitt Pickett, Lead Developer for the condominium, asked Austin Cook for his opinion as one of the next generation of Mountview residents.
>
> Austin replied that "chopping off the top of a beautiful mountain would be like taking a beautiful girl and giving her a flat top."
>
> That image, which speaks volumes, will surely be a focal point for Tuesday's meeting at the Town Hall.

Uncle Steve put down the paper and said, "Our local hero just created quite a stir. Could that be what people are talking about?"

Our breakfast arrived and we tried to eat in silence. I wasn't looking at anyone now. I just wanted to eat quietly and then go hide. Suddenly, it wasn't such fun to have people know who I was.

We finished breakfast, and as Uncle Steve paid the bill, the owner pointed at Uncle Steve's newspaper, which was folded so that you could see the picture of the haircut.

"Is that your opinion, too?" he asked.

"Yeah, pretty much," Uncle Steve answered.

As we walked out he said to us, "You know, this whole issue has a way of making people pick sides. It's sad to see, but unavoidable."

We drove over to the Nature Museum. Uncle Steve dropped us off, honked, and then drove away.

"Sarah sent me a message!" I blurted as I walked into the Museum and saw Amy.

"Well, good morning to you, too, Austin." Amy glanced at Katie and asked, "Does Katie know about all this?"

"Yes, pretty much. I told her awhile ago when it first happened."

"OK, what did Sarah say?" Amy asked.

"She didn't just say something. She said she needed my help and to come as soon as I could. Her message hit me real hard, like an explosion. Now, I am really worried," I said.

"Was there any more to the message?" Amy asked.

"Nothing more, it just ended. What do you think is happening? How do we get in touch with her? What should we do next?" My words tumbled over each other.

"Hold on just a second. Let's think this through," Amy said calmly. "Do you know where Sarah is?"

"No," I said flatly.

"Do you know anything more about what the problem is?" Amy asked.

"No," I replied, shaking my head.

"OK, so we don't know anything except that she's in trouble," Amy concluded. "So let's go find her. I didn't have much we needed to do today anyway. Why don't we all do this together? We can start by going to the areas where we know Sarah has been before. We will look at the release zone. Then we can go look over at the caves at Mill Creek. Let's get started."

"Let's go," I agreed.

The Suburban started with a roar, and in a minute we were on the road. As we drove through town I looked at the various stores and shops that lined Main Street. Something caught my eye in one of the store windows that we passed. We were going slowly enough that I quickly looked behind me. I saw the store and looked in the window at a poster sitting in plain view. *Oh no, it can't be.* I turned around and let it sink in. I was pretty sure I had seen a poster of a woman with a flat top.

Amy slowed down, for no apparent reason, and then she pulled into one of the many angled parking slots that lined Main Street and turned the car off. I was looking around trying to figure out why she stopped.

Amy said, "Austin, do you see what I see?"

I looked at Amy to see where she was looking. In the window of the shop to the right of us was a poster of a woman with her hair cut in a flat top.

"Oh my goodness," Amy said.

Katie was laughing. "Austin, there's your girlfriend."

Without taking my eyes off the poster, I opened the door and got out of the Suburban. I slowly walked up to the window. I believe my mouth was wide open. As I stared at the poster in disbelief, I read the words that were next to the picture. 'A vote for the building project will get us all clipped. Vote NO and save our environment.' I heard two car doors close and was joined by Amy and Katie. All three of us were staring at the poster. Not a word was said.

The silence was broken when the door of the shop opened and a woman, noticing that we were looking in her window, walked out to us. She said, "Well what do you think? Is that a good poster or what?"

None of us spoke.

She continued as if she knew we needed an explanation. "Jamie Little stayed up late last night and printed a mess of these. Isn't it great? He's out delivering them all over town."

Amy looked at the woman and said, "What do you mean, delivering them all over town?"

The woman said, "A bunch of us who don't want that condo built have been waiting for something to rally around. We are going to put these all over town. You're Austin, aren't you?" she asked as she turned away from Amy and looked at me.

I nodded my head.

"Well, yesterday you said what was on all our minds so we decided to print these up and get organized. You know, a picture is worth a thousand words. We'll stop this thing yet." She was smiling. "Thanks for the idea. You've got us going now, and we appreciate it."

"You're welcome," I said.

We walked back to the Suburban. Amy started the engine and remarked, "This is going to get interesting."

Chapter 8

We continued our drive to the release zone. I stopped thinking about the poster and got back to thinking about Sarah. I was 'listening' very closely, trying to pick up any signal from her. I was also talking out loud, trying to communicate back to her.

"Austin, what are you saying?" Katie asked.

"I'm trying to talk to Sarah," I replied, keeping my mind on what I was doing.

"She isn't in the car. Why don't you stick you head outside the car? Then she might be able to hear you," she suggested.

"You don't understand. Just be quiet."

When we arrived at the release zone I jumped out first. I walked around the area, saying, "Sarah, can you hear me now? Can you hear me now?"

I turned to Amy. "I think I need to go further into the woods. Do you want to come with me?"

"Yes, give me a moment, and then we can all go." Amy returned to the Suburban to get her compass. After locking the car, she joined Katie and me. "OK, let's go back into the woods using the trail along Mills Creek."

We entered the woods. Mills Creek was flowing briskly due to the recent rain. The further we walked into the woods, the louder the sounds of the forest became. The distinctive peaceful sounds of the creek, as its water gently tumbled over the rocks, were periodically interrupted by me talking loudly, trying to get Sarah's attention. Amy and Katie walked in silence but were constantly looking for any sign of a skunk.

Then I stopped in my tracks. I heard a faint sound. I moved my head back and forth, trying to get a better feel for where it was coming from.

"I've got her!" I yelled.

Then I said, "Sarah, I'm near the release zone, are you close by?"

For Amy and Katie is must have been like listening to one end of a telephone conversation. They only heard me speaking, but they could tell I was definitely hearing the other end of the conversation; they could see it in my eyes.

"Yes, I'm with Amy and Katie and we'll meet you at the release zone," I said out loud.

I spun around and looked at Katie and Amy, "Let's go back to the zone. Sarah will meet us there very soon." We hurried back the way we had come.

Back at the release zone, Amy sat on a log with Katie, waiting. Occasionally, Amy said something to keep Katie occupied. I was pacing back and forth, only a few feet away from them.

I stopped walking and asked, "Why didn't she tell me where she was?"

It was a question, but I didn't direct the question to them.

I resumed walking back and forth. I stopped again and asked, "Why did she wait this long to call me? I've been here for a few days. She could have called me when I arrived."

I started pacing back and forth again. Amy and Katie stopped what they were doing and just watched me, their heads pivoting as I walked back and forth right in front of them.

I stopped. "Couldn't she have used long distance or something?" I held that thought for a moment and then continued my pacing.

Amy looked over at Katie and shrugged her shoulders.

Katie said, "Austin, who are you talking to?"

I didn't even acknowledge her. I just kept moving. But then I stopped for a moment, raised my arm and pointed upward. Without saying anything, I dropped my arm and started pacing again.

Katie looked at Amy, leaned over to get just a little closer and whispered, "He's a very troubled young man."

Amy looked shocked for a moment and then realized how funny all this was. She began to laugh and then Katie began to laugh. They were laughing loud enough to get me to stop in my tracks for a moment. I just stared at them.

I said, "I can't believe this. Sarah is in trouble and you two are laughing about it. What kind of people are you?"

With that, Katie stopped to catch her breath for a moment. "Normal ones!" she shouted, and then they started laughing even louder.

I looked at Katie and then at Amy. I shook my head and started to pace again.

Amy stopped laughing and said to me, "We aren't laughing about Sarah - we are worried about her, too. We're also worried about you. We need everyone to be calm, Austin. We need you to stop pacing and maintain your mental and physical strength. You're forgetting your survival training."

That last statement caught my attention. I hadn't noticed what I was doing. Amy was exactly correct. I had let my emotions take over. One of the rules of survival was to keep your senses. I stopped my pacing and stood still, looking at the ground in front of me.

"You're right." I kicked the dirt in front of me. "I'm just worried."

"We're all worried, but we can't do anything about it at this time. Let's stop, relax the best we can, and conserve our strength. We'll need to act quickly when Sarah arrives. Don't you agree?"

I looked up and caught Amy's eyes. I then looked around one more time to see if Sarah had arrived. I didn't see any signs of her. "You're right. I'll conserve my strength."

After another moment, I stepped toward the log. Katie moved closer to Amy which gave me the room I needed to sit down.

"Thanks," I said, easing myself onto the log.

Katie reached out and patted me on the shoulder. She didn't say anything, just offered an affectionate pat on the shoulder, as if to say, 'I care.'

I appreciated the gesture.

It was probably twenty minutes later, although it felt like hours, when Sarah finally arrived.

There was some rustling in a nearby bush; nothing particularly loud, but louder than normal. That noise attracted our attention. Our individual activities at that moment, which consisted mostly of independent thought, stopped as we all directed our attention to the brush off to our right. Suddenly, a rather robust raccoon rumbled out of the thicket toward us. We were startled, not by the aggressive nature of the animal, but by the shock of seeing a raccoon and not a skunk. Any fear was quickly replaced with relief when each of us noticed the animal tag dancing in the sun as the raccoon moved through a patch of sunlight.

"Sarah!" I yelled and ran toward the raccoon. Amy and Katie stood to watch.

Sarah rumbled towards me. When we were almost together, I leaned down and she leaped into my arms. I wrapped my arms around her and gave her a hug. Amy and Katie walked toward us.

I rubbed my face in her coat and laughed when Sarah sent, *'You are lucky I ran **around** the poison ivy patch.'*

I said out loud, "I don't care, I missed you."

Amy and Katie were now right next to me. Katie said, "Group hug," and all four of us locked in an embrace.

After a few precious moments, Amy said, "This is great, but don't we have an emergency on our hands?"

It was clear that no one – not Amy, Katie, me, not even Sarah – wanted to stop our bonding. But we all knew there was a big problem that needed to be solved, so we reluctantly released each other and Amy, Katie and I looked at Sarah expectantly.

Sarah sent, *'I have been with the raccoons over near Lake Minti. My raccoon friends are sick, and some are so sick that they are slowly dying.*

65

I have been helping them move to other areas, but the water is getting really bad. One of them is with me. She is waiting in the brush.'

I said out loud, "We know that the lake is getting contaminated, but no one knows where it's coming from."

'Well, I know,' Sarah sent. *'It all started with DeWitt Pickett's property. He has been leaking poisons into Jackson's Stream for a long time. No one has stopped it. Jackson's Stream flows into the lake. The animals drink from the lake and the stream and they are getting sick. If the lake gets any worse, we will all be fighting for our lives.'*

I relayed the information to Amy.

"Pickett!" she exclaimed. "Can Sarah take us to the source?"

I asked Sarah, "Can you take us there, so we can see for ourselves?"

'Yes, but there are always people walking around the property. We will have to be careful. It could be dangerous.'

I relayed that information and Amy said, "I imagine Mr. Pickett knows that people are looking for the source of the contaminants and he will stop at nothing to protect it. Sarah is right; we'll have to be very careful."

I repeated this to Sarah, who sent, *'It is getting too late to find it today. Let's meet at your house at dawn.'*

Amy agreed and added, "Good idea. We'll put Sarah in a car cage and if anyone asks, we will say we're releasing her into the forest. We'll simply release her on Pickett's property. If anyone sees us, we should be able to talk our way out of it."

So that was the plan. Sarah agreed and said she would meet us. She sent, *'I need to go back with my friend. I will see you tomorrow, Austin.'* And with that she rubbed up against my leg and scurried into the forest.

I watched and called out, "Be careful, Sarah."

She turned and gave me one last look. At that point I saw the other raccoon stick her head out of the brush as if to say, *'Come on, we need to go.'* And then they both disappeared into the brush.

* * * * *

Not far away, a lone dark figure was standing on the porch of an old house located deep in the forest. The road leading to the house was as mysterious as the figure standing next to it. Although the sun was still shining as it sank across the sky, the many trees of the forest blocked most of the sun's rays, casting sinister shadows across the house and across the face of the man who owned the property. He leaned against a wooden railing that was in need of a coat of paint. His dark and sunken eyes were gazing through the trees, across a large farm pond, to a nearby mountain.

DeWitt Pickett was a very unpleasant fellow. It was not that he had to be. It was not that he should be. It was what he *chose* to be. He knew circumstances might take away his freedom and his money. He must stop that at all costs. All he needed was a little time. He must protect himself long enough to have the building project started so that he could completely get rid of the evidence. He knew that various government agencies and environmental activists were looking for the source of the contaminants, which meant they were looking for him. He knew they wouldn't stop. So he had his men waiting to catch anyone who got close to his property. He had a trap set for anyone who might just stumble upon it. He could relax.

The slightly bent figure made his way back into the dark confines of his house. The shadows that fell upon the house were reminiscent of the past, before Mountview was a flourishing town, when DeWitt was just a boy. He was reminded of his father, how hard he had worked to build a life for his family. His father hadn't known what harm he was causing by having chemicals stored on his property. Actually, DeWitt remembered that when his father had expressed concern it had been about running the still they had operated inside a mountain cave. But oddly enough the still, although illegal, was not the problem these days. The problem was those drums of chemicals.

DeWitt's father had made much of his fortune by allowing chemicals to be stored in the mountain that was located on his property. Companies had saved a lot of money by disposing of their waste products that way, rather than hauling them to distant disposal sites or processing them to convert them to harmless substances. But the world had changed, and having those chemicals around was no longer considered an innocent act.

The United States Environmental Protection Agency had become a force to be reckoned with, constantly searching for hazardous substances in its zeal to protect people. Pickett knew that those storage drums, once found, would be his ruin. He had to get rid of them.

His first idea had been to dump them into his farm pond. He remembered the day he had decided to do just that. His men took about 50 drums, opened them, and dumped their contents into the pond. He figured his fish would get sick and perhaps die. But what did he care? He didn't eat the fish; let them die. He figured some of the animals that drank from the pond might get sick. But so what? *Who cares if a few animals get sick and die, there are a lot more where they came from,* he had told himself. But what he hadn't figured on was that the pond would leak into Jackson Stream, and that the stream would leak into Lake Minti. And he certainly didn't figure that Lake Minti would get polluted.

After that, he hadn't done any more dumping. But that had left him with a doubly dangerous dilemma. There were many, many storage drums on his property that were still filled with their harmful contents. And now the contaminants discovered in the lake had alerted the authorities that there were hazardous chemicals somewhere in the area, so unless he did something to stop them, it was only a matter of time before they tracked down the source. He'd realized that he had to come up with another plan.

Then one day, the idea became a vision. Several architects had approached him to talk about the building project. He smiled. That was a great plan. The project would be good for the town, and it would be very good for him. Once he got approval for the project – and he *would* get approval for the building project – they would dig deep holes for the building's foundation. And then, under the cover of darkness, he would dump his barrels deep into the holes, put concrete on top of them, and no one would ever know. Yes, that was a great idea.

All he needed was to get the approval for the high-rise, then truck the barrels from the mountain and put them into the foundation his crews would dig. After that, he would deal with the pond, and his problems would be solved. All he had to do was to get the building project approved. And he controlled just about every aspect of the plan; all except one - public opinion.

He had controlled public opinion until that Austin kid showed up. Now, he wasn't so sure. But the kid was only twelve years old. Surely, a man of DeWitt's experience and stature in the community could control a twelve-year-old kid.

Surely....

Chapter 9

Tuesday morning came quickly.

The night before, Amy, Katie, and I had told Uncle Steve about our plan. He was not in favor of it at all. He agreed that something needed to be done, but he thought that sneaking onto someone's property was too dangerous. We disagreed. Amy argued that we needed proof before we could make allegations and, quite frankly, that we weren't even sure where on Mr. Pickett's property the poison was coming from. We also knew that we would have one chance to prove it and if we missed the first time, we might not get another chance. Just as important, we believed that Mr. Pickett's eagerness to get the building project approved so quickly, meant that he intended to use that project to somehow cover up the environmental problem.

Uncle Steve reluctantly agreed with our arguments. He wanted to go with us. However, he had booked an appointment with the County Commissioner almost three weeks earlier, and could not cancel it. So Uncle Steve, although not happy, had grudgingly agreed to our plan.

Amy was at the door at five thirty in the morning, just as planned. Katie and I had just finished dressing and were on our way down the stairs. This time, I had used an alarm clock and put it under my pillow. Sarah was waiting on the deck without her companion from the day before. Katie and I walked through the kitchen to the back door.

"What's that clanking noise?" I asked.

"That's my flashlight," Katie replied.

"We can use my flashlight. Yours is making too much noise."

"You aren't the only one who gets to have a flashlight. I get one, too."

I opened the back door, where Sarah and Amy were waiting. "Listen, you guys, can you hear how much noise her flashlight is making? Katie, you're going to wake the entire town. Please leave the flashlight here."

Amy realized what was happening and said, "Austin, Katie will keep her flashlight very quiet, won't you Katie?"

"Yes, Austin, I will keep *my* flashlight very quiet."

I didn't say anything else. I walked off the deck toward the car and the others followed. The Suburban was unlocked and the animal cage was ready for occupancy. I lifted Sarah into the cage while Amy and Katie got in the car.

"Hi Sarah," I said as I placed her gently into the cage.

'Hi Austin,' she sent. *'Thanks for the lift.'*

In a matter of minutes we were packed up and headed down the highway to Mr. Pickett's property.

We parked the car just off the road about a half mile from the entrance to Mr. Pickett's land. Up to this point, no one had seen us. So far, so good. I walked behind the vehicle, calmly looked around, opened the tailgate and the cage, and helped Sarah onto the ground.

We walked down the road a short distance, then veered off toward the pond. Instead of walking along Mr. Pickett's driveway, which might alert someone to our presence, Amy guided us through the trees to a clearing. The tree line would lead us toward the south side of the pond. Once we reached the pond, we planned to check out the area and then work our way over to Jackson's Stream.

Amy checked her compass, then led the way followed by Katie, then me. We stayed within the cover of the trees, skirting the edge of the clearing. Sarah rambled slightly ahead of the group, but she would occasionally catch a scent and then go off in another direction to check it out. When she had satisfied her curiosity, she would reappear and join us. We were making good progress along the tree line heading to the pond. Again, so far, so good.

Sarah sent me a message, *'I smell something over to the east of us. I will check it out, talk to some animal friends, and meet up with you later.'* And with that, she was gone.

Amy continued to lead Katie and me. The darkness was slowly fading away. Amy was able to pack her compass away, since she was now relying on sight. After a few more minutes we caught our first glimpse of the pond and the buildings near it. I unclipped my flashlight from my belt so it would be handy when we reached the first building.

The sun was beginning to light the sky, illuminating the pond. Amy had reached the edge of the trees and was about to lead us into the open, around the pond to the outbuildings located along the west side of the water. But before we moved away from the trees she wanted to make certain that no one was around. We stopped under a large oak tree, crouching behind it so we would not be seen. The three of us looked around cautiously. Sarah had not returned yet.

"We'll walk over to that small red building, the one closest to us, and then we'll stop," Amy whispered. She looked at each of us to make sure we were paying close attention, then continued. "Remember to move quietly and don't say anything until we get there, OK?"

Katie and I nodded our heads and stood up. As we walked across the clearing, we kept a close watch around us, looking from side to side to make certain that we didn't see anything out of the ordinary. I didn't like the fact that Sarah had not returned, but I made myself stay focused on what we were doing.

It seemed like it took us forever to reach the first building. Once there, we hid in the shadows while Amy opened the door to look inside. The door made a noise as she opened it; probably the hinges needed some oil. I turned on my flashlight and flashed the beam into the building so we could see what was inside. We scanned the interior. Nothing of interest there. It was nearly empty except for a few paint cans, some rags, and something that smelled like oil or gas.

When she was satisfied, Amy motioned for me to turn off the light, then she slowly closed the door. "Nothing in here," she whispered. "Now let's go over to that building there."

She pointed to a larger red building about twenty yards away. The sun was rising and the light was making everything, including us, more visible. I kept looking around to make certain that no one was on to us. Amy motioned for us to follow and we did.

We were about halfway to the building when Katie stumbled and fell over something in the field. I don't know what it was, but when she fell, her flashlight, which up to now had been quietly hanging on her belt, made a loud clanking noise as it bounced against her belt buckle. I pulled her up and we ran to the next building, clanking all the way. Once there, we ducked into the shadows and waited to see if the noise had awakened anyone. We didn't see or hear anything.

"What was that about? Give me that flashlight," I demanded, grabbing for it.

"No! I get to carry the flashlight. Amy?" Katie cried.

"Would you guys be quiet?" Amy commanded in an urgent whisper. "May I have the flashlight, Katie? Are you all right?"

"Yeah, but why can't I keep the flashlight? You said I could," Katie whined.

"That was before you and your brother started waking the dead." Amy reached out and took the flashlight. "Now, let's stay focused here." Her voice was quiet, but firm. I looked down, suddenly embarrassed.

"What do you mean, the dead?" Katie asked.

"Just a figure of speech. Try not to make any more noise, OK?"

"Yeah. But what's this about the dead?" Katie persisted.

Amy laid a finger across Katie's lips to silence her, waited until she was sure Katie was still, then she turned away to open the door of the second building. She reached for, then found, the latch. As the door started to move there was a slight sound of squeaky hinges. Amy put the flashlight she had taken from Katie on the ground and opened the door very slowly, using both hands. I was kneeling at the corner of the building, looking back in the direction we had come from to make certain that we weren't being followed. Katie's clanking flashlight had seemed louder to me than my alarm clock.

When the door was finally opened, Amy picked up the flashlight and pointed it into the building. It didn't look like there was much inside, but this building was larger than the first so the light wasn't strong enough for her to see everything clearly. She motioned for us to follow her as she stepped through the doorway.

Once we were safely inside, Amy cautiously pushed the door closed so nobody outside would see the open door and come to investigate. Katie and I stood motionless, our eyes fixed on Amy, trying not to make a sound. When the door was finally closed, I heard three sighs of relief and realized that we had all been holding our breath. It felt very good to be safely hidden.

Amy turned and started to shine her light around the room. The flashlight's beam fell on something along the wall only a few feet away. It appeared to be a large object covered by a tarp. It must have been hidden from view by the door when she looked in from outside. The narrow flashlight beam revealed only a small portion of whatever it was, since the object was so close. Puzzled, she slowly moved the beam higher to see more of the object. She still couldn't figure it out, nor could we. She raised the beam higher, higher, and then higher. Suddenly, too late, she realized what she was seeing.

Amy gasped, Katie screamed, and I jumped back, hitting the inside wall of the building.

The beam had reached a face – a man's very large unshaven face – revealing his wide open eyes and an unpleasant smile displaying several missing teeth. The man quickly stepped to the side, so that his massive body blocked the door. Before we could move, all hope of escape had disappeared. There was a click and the inside of the red building became bright with light. The overhead bulb was weak but gave off enough light for us to wince as we stared at the large man who was blocking our exit.

After glaring at us for a moment he spoke in a low, raspy voice. "Good morning, ladies, nice of you to drop by. Won't you sit down and stay for awhile?"

We sank to the floor near the center of the building, huddling together. Amy sat between Katie and me, keeping a reassuring arm around each of us. The tall, hairy man leaned against the door and stared at us without saying another word. He didn't need to speak. His stare was scary enough. His white T-shirt was soiled, and there were wet areas by his underarms. His big arms were hairy, sweaty and very long. His large size, his black straggly, uncombed hair, and his very large head reminded me of a big, ugly gorilla – fierce, mean and unpredictable. There was a foul odor, which may have been the old building or it may have been him. I didn't want to get close enough to find out.

After a minute, Amy cleared her throat as if to say something. Before she could get it out, she was interrupted by a knock on the door. The scary man opened it. Entering the confines of the dimly lighted building was none other than Mr. DeWitt Pickett himself.

"Well, isn't this a surprise," he said softly as the door closed behind him. "Look who we have here. Our very own Park Ranger. Just making sure we don't have any sick animals out here, is that what you're doing?" he continued, directing his comments to Amy.

She said, "No, actually we were out here releasing one of our animals. We just released the animal and we were on our way back to the car."

"Oh, you were, were you? So where is the cage? And, oh, by the way, what time is it? Isn't it a bit early for animal releases?"

"No, actually…" Amy began.

"'No, actually,' *what*?" he demanded. "You are trespassing on my property. It is a crime to trespass. Didn't anyone ever tell you that?"

Without waiting for a response, Mr. Pickett continued, speaking more slowly. "You know, it's quite dark out there. Dangerously dark." He paused for a moment, then pretended to be talking to a policeman. "Honestly, officer, I couldn't tell who or what it was. I shot my gun in self-defense." He paused, waiting for his words to sink in. "I am so sorry that I shot them all…*dead*."

Katie began to cry. Amy held her closer and said fiercely, "Don't you scare the children!"

"You had better be thinking of more than just me scaring the children. You'd better be thinking of staying alive!"

Katie was now crying loudly. I jumped up, ready to defend us, but the big gorilla pushed me back to the floor.

"This isn't a breakfast party, kiddies," Mr. Pickett went on, his eyes flashing angrily. "This is real life crime. You are trespassing on my land and I have the right to protect my property. You are in real trouble."

Mr. Pickett paused. He looked at Katie and then settled his icy gaze on me. He moved closer until he was almost touching me. I had to tilt my head back to keep my eyes on his face.

"So we have the 'town hero' with us this morning," he said. "The big town hero should have kept his mouth shut. We may have to help him with that."

"You'd better not harm him. He's a child," Amy warned.

Mr. Pickett raised his hand as if he was going to slap Amy, but at the last moment he stopped himself and dropped his hand. "Enough from you," he told her sharply, "I will do anything I want."

He noticed her compass case. "And the first thing I will do is take this equipment. Give me that compass, your knives, and those flashlights. All that stuff," he ordered. We reluctantly handed over our gear.

Looking back at me, Mr. Pickett spoke quietly, as if thinking out loud. "Yes, you need to keep your mouth shut. You need to keep your mouth shut all day. That's right. The town meeting is tonight and if you aren't there…better yet, if you are *all* not there, then my chances of winning the vote will improve significantly."

He paused. He stared at the ceiling intently. He turned and slowly walked to the other side of the small building.

"Hmmm. Yes, that's it." He stopped and turned back to us. "Make yourselves comfortable, won't you?" He then directed his words to the big, ugly guy, but still looked at us. "Mr. Jones, make our guests comfortable. We will have the pleasure of their company for the rest of the day."

Mr. Pickett walked over to Mr. Jones and whispered a few words, just out of our hearing range. He stared at me for a few moments, whispered something more to Mr. Jones, then exited. The menacing Mr. Jones stayed, resuming his position against the door.

"What does he mean when he says 'the rest of the day'…Mr. Jones?" Amy asked.

In a low, frightening voice, Mr. Jones said, "You will stay here until the town meeting is over. Then you will be free to leave. Unless you cause trouble, that is." Mr. Jones began to smile and I noticed several teeth were

75

missing. "If you cause any trouble I have the authority to do anything necessary." He laughed quietly. It was a very unsettling sound.

The only source of light in the small building was from the overhead bulb and a window that faced north, toward the pond. *First things first,* I thought, and scanned the building for a more comfortable place to sit. To my surprise, I spotted a wooden chair.

"Mr. Jones? May I bring that chair over here for Amy and Katie?" I asked.

Mr. Jones looked over as if he hadn't noticed the chair before.

"No, boy," he said, "but if you know what's good for you, you'll bring it over to me."

I sighed. That hadn't worked out well. I stood up, stretched out the aches that had already developed from sitting on the hard floor, and then dragged the chair toward Mr. Jones. I left it a few feet in front of him, not wanting to get within his reach. He laughed at me, clearly enjoying my discomfort, and pulled the chair to him. After pushing it close to the door he sat down and leaned back. He looked far too comfortable for my taste. *Maybe he'll fall asleep,* I thought. Only one problem with that plan. Since he's leaning against the only exit, we still couldn't get out.

Resuming my inspection, I noticed a board propped up by several large bricks. It was being used as a shelf to hold a few cans and other items, but it was mostly empty and looked strong enough to hold us.

"May we sit over there?" I asked Mr. Jones, and pointed to the board.

He shrugged and motioned us to go ahead.

Amy and Katie got stiffly to their feet, stretched for a moment, then we moved to the makeshift bench, making ourselves as comfortable as possible. It wasn't much, but it was a lot better than the cold, dirty floor. I settled in to take a careful inventory of our surroundings.

The building looked old and worn. Several aging boards had splintered and broken at the base where the floor and the walls met. The sun was still low, but provided enough light to filter into the building through the cracks. One hole was large enough to see grass outside. That was all I could see, except for the patch of sky visible through the small window.

Shelves, scattered irregularly along the walls, held various small items. I noticed several old cans of paint, some spray cans – perhaps ant and roach killer – and several empty glass Mason jars used for canning. A few tools leaned against the wall. I saw a rickety garden rake, a trowel, and in the corner a stack of rags. *Nothing noteworthy,* I thought. *Nothing that might help us escape.*

Escape. That is exactly what was going through my mind. We had to escape. I stole a look at Amy. She was holding Katie, gently stroking her hair. Katie had quieted but she was still very frightened. Amy was thinking, I could see that. Between the two of us, we would have to figure out how to escape. But how?

Chapter 10

I tried to think of a clever plan, but my thoughts kept drifting to the town meeting that would take place at seven o'clock that night. It would be the most important meeting that Mountview had ever had. This would be the townspeople's only chance to officially share what they thought about the proposed high-rise before the Town Council voted on the building project. Once the Council approved the high-rise, there wouldn't be anything more we could do to stop it. Mr. Pickett would get exactly what he wanted.

Amy broke the silence. "Mr. Jones, I have to use the bathroom."

Good idea, I thought.

Mr. Jones said, "Mr. Pickett said that you would ask that." Mr. Jones opened the door. The view was blocked, but I could hear him mumbling to someone outside. That was bad. I wondered if there was more than one person guarding the door from outside.

"You can go, but the kids stay," Mr. Jones told Amy.

"Well, Katie needs to use the bathroom and I'm sure that Austin needs to."

"They stay. You go," Mr. Jones insisted.

Amy looked at Katie and said, "You sit over here with Austin and I'll go first. I'll be right back. It's all right."

Katie slid over, keeping a fearful eye on Mr. Jones. She snuggled against me. I wondered if that was for warmth or comfort. Once Katie was settled, Amy stood and moved to the door. Mr. Jones opened it a crack so she could see the person he had spoken with.

"This is Mr. Smith," Mr. Jones growled. "Do exactly as he says."

Mr. Smith was a small, plump person. He needed a shave, and looked as if he had not changed his clothes in days.

"You," said Mr. Smith rudely to Amy. "Come with me."

Mr. Jones watched as Mr. Smith led Amy away from the building. Then he closed the door behind them and turned his stare to Katie and me. Katie wiggled even closer to me and buried her face against my shoulder so she couldn't see Mr. Jones. Part of me wanted to do that, too, but I knew that kind of escape wasn't going to help us.

* * * * *

Amy and Mr. Smith walked across the field toward a very small building. As they approached Amy could see that it was an outhouse. It must have been left over from the old days when it would have been the only bathroom on the farm.

Mr. Smith opened the door with a flourish and said, "Here you are. I am sure you will be quite comfortable. If you need any help, just let me know."

As a taunting smile came over his face, Amy could see that his teeth were badly stained and his gums looked unhealthy. *Odd,* Amy thought as she entered the darkness, *they sure could use a good dental plan up here.*

The distinctive smells that always accompany an outhouse were present. Although it was dark and smelly, it wasn't too frightening. Amy looked around the inside of the small building and couldn't find any clues for escape. She noticed a roll of toilet tissue. *Beats using a page from the Sears Catalog,* she thought.

There was a tap on the door and she heard Mr. Smith saying, "Do you find everything you need?" Clearly, he was finding the situation quite entertaining. Amy forced herself to keep her temper. Getting into an argument with a guard could only make things worse.

"Yes, thank you, I'll be out in a moment," she replied.

A few minutes later, Amy opened the door and exited the outhouse. Mr. Smith ordered her to walk back to the building while he followed. She obeyed, walking slowly and casually surveying the surroundings. When Mr. Jones heard them approach, he moved his chair aside and opened the door. Amy went inside; Mr. Smith stayed outside. *Everyone back to your appointed corners,* she thought.

* * * * *

Amy sat down on our board bench and asked if either one of us needed to use the bathroom. Katie was still too frightened to leave Amy and me. I was too busy concentrating on escape.

There was a slight tap on the door. Mr. Jones stood up and once again moved his chair aside. Mr. Pickett stepped into the building.

"So, how are you enjoying my hospitality?" he asked in his deep, rich voice, sounding for all the world as if we were his favorite guests at a party.

Amy looked at him. "We're hungry and we want to go home."

Mr. Pickett said, "Well you can go home anytime you want, Miss Park Ranger, but the children stay...by themselves. I'm certain that Mr. Smith and Mr. Jones will be glad to entertain them."

"You're disgusting."

"Yes, well, sticks and stones..." he mimicked like a child. "I will be leaving you now. Oh, did you hear there is a town meeting this evening? I will be there. You won't." He smiled. "Too bad. My two associates will see that you stay here to enjoy our hospitality for the rest of the day. However, just in case by some chance you manage to slip away, I thought I should let you know that I moved your car. It could have been a danger to someone traveling this back road, don't you think? You could say I did the county a favor. You can thank me later. By the way, I moved your car to the edge of town. That way, no one will know that you were even here.

"So you see, if you do manage to escape," he continued, "your walk back to town will take you most of the day. In other words, Parkie, you won't make it in time...if you make it at all." Mr. Pickett laughed confidently and turned to walk away. He stopped and turned back. "Oh, by the way, I plan to name the new high-rise after you three. I am calling it 'Nashew Iunnee.' It means, too little, too late."

He laughed and walked to the door, saying, "Mr. Jones will let you go Wednesday morning. Of course, it will be too late for you to do anything about the building project. And if you say that I held you here, I'll call you liars. After all, you didn't attend the biggest meeting this town has ever had. Of course, you would make up an excuse about why you let *all* your friends down by not showing up." As Mr. Pickett walked away we could still hear him repeating, "Too little, too late, ha ha ha ha." The door closed.

The sound of the door closing was like the final nail being driven into the coffin. Katie started to cry again. Amy tried to comfort her. I was thinking and thinking, and then it hit me. *Where is Sarah?* I had completely forgotten about her. *All I need to do is to talk to Sarah and she will help,* I thought.

I started to speak quietly. "Can you hear me?"

Mr. Jones looked over at me.

I repeated, "Can you hear me?"

Mr. Jones said, "Prayer may be your only way out, boy. But you better keep them prayers to yourself. Now, shut up!"

My eyes were wide open, staring at Mr. Jones. The last thing I wanted to do was to make this big man angry, so I stopped talking, but kept thinking. *How can I communicate with Sarah?*

Amy could see what was happening. She was thinking of a plan. She said, "Mr. Jones, it is obvious that Austin needs to use the bathroom."

Mr. Jones looked at me from head to toe, sizing me up.

I realized what Amy was suggesting. "Yes sir. I was just trying not to think of having to go, so I was talking out loud. May I use the bathroom… please, sir?"

Mr. Jones said, "You have to stop talking, so do what you have to do. Go on then, and come back quickly."

Mr. Jones stood and opened the door. Mr. Smith was sitting outside the door. He rose and watched me come outside. The door closed behind me. Mr. Smith guided me to the outhouse, as he had Amy. He watched me go inside, telling me, "Hurry up."

I entered and closed the door behind me. Once inside I focused on my mission. I spoke out loud, "Sarah, can you hear me?" I paused for a moment, then said, "Where are you? Sarah, can you hear me?" I stopped and listened.

Mr. Smith spoke, "Yes, I can hear you. Now shut up and do your business or I will come in there and drag you out myself."

I said, "I'm just so nervous, I can't pee. I won't be long. Just let me talk myself through this."

Mr. Smith laughed. He obviously thought I was a pretty weird kid. He repeated, more forcefully, "Hurry up!"

I said, "Sarah! Sarah!"

Then all of a sudden, I heard *'I am here. I have found the source. It is the pond. It is full of contamination. Where are you?'*

"I'm at the outhouse. You can't miss the smell; it's easy to find. We need your help."

Mr. Smith interrupted, "You've got one more minute."

I continued, "We're being held captive by two of Pickett's men. We need your help. Come quickly."

Mr. Smith pounded on the door, "Ready or not, here I come!" He opened the door, took my arm, and pulled me outside.

I was escorted back to the building. Suddenly, I saw Sarah! She scurried across the path several feet ahead of Mr. Smith and me, her tag flopping back and forth.

"Get outta here," Mr. Smith yelled, "you good-for-nothing varmint!"

Sarah ran into the nearby brush. I smiled, my confidence restored. Sarah was safe, she was back, and she was free.

I went back into the building and sat on the bench. I smiled at Mr. Jones, then smiled at Amy and Katie.

Mr. Jones gave me an odd look and asked, "Does it make you that happy every time you go to the bathroom?"

I thought for a moment, wanting to use this chance to talk to get a message to Amy. I said, "We're all worried, but we can't do anything about it at this time. Let's relax the best we can and conserve our strength. We'll need to act quickly when Sarah arrives. Don't you agree?"

Mr. Jones tilted his head and looked at me in amazement. "What's wrong with you kids these days?"

Amy understood me. She gave Katie a little hug and said casually, "I see what you mean. I think everything will be fine."

Sarah sent a message. *'I know you can't send to me without talking out loud. You know, you really need to work on that. For the time being, I will send to you. I am going for help. Stay calm. I will be back soon.'*

"I will be here," I said to Sarah without realizing what I was doing.

"Stop your yapping, already!" ordered Mr. Jones.

"Sorry, sorry, it won't happen again, sorry," I said. Then I turned slightly toward Amy and Katie and gave a slight wink.

It must have been just a few minutes later when we got the first sign that something was beginning to happen. It was, of all things, a crow calling. I recognized it immediately. 'Caw-Caw-Caw,' then it repeated, 'Caw-Caw-Caw.'

The raucous call broke the morning silence. I sensed that this was the beginning of the help that Sarah had pursued. Again, we heard 'Caw-Caw-Caw,' very loudly now as if the crow was right on top of the building. Mr. Jones glanced up at the ceiling. The crowing increased. Now it was coming from two, maybe three crows that were right on top of the building. Mr. Jones was still looking up. He stood up, grabbed the rake, and pounded the handle against the roof. With that, the crows flew off and there was silence. After listening for a moment with the rake poised in his hand, Mr. Jones was satisfied that the birds were gone. He replaced the rake and returned to his chair.

Before long the crows resumed their calling. Now, the sounds were at a distance but they seemed to have increased in number. Soon the crowing seemed to be all around us.

There was a tap at the door. We heard Mr. Smith's voice. "Uh, Mr. Jones? Something is going on out here."

"Yeah, yeah. It's just some birds. Relax," Mr. Jones said without moving from his chair.

The cawing continued. Mr. Jones moved his head around as if he was trying to determine what direction the sounds were coming from and what had started such a ruckus.

There was another tap on the door. Mr. Smith's voice was more urgent now. "Mr. Jones, you really need to come see this."

Mr. Jones stood up so he could get a better angle on the view through the window at the back of the building. He didn't see anything out of the ordinary. Then he saw a raccoon run across his line of sight, about twenty feet from the window.

"It's a raccoon, for God's sake! Get a hold of yourself!" he exclaimed, shaking his head in disgust.

Mr. Jones returned to his chair. He sat down and stared at us as if he was daring us to say something. We avoided meeting his eyes and stayed very quiet. The cawing continued.

A few minutes later there was a frantic knock on the door and we heard Mr. Smith say, "If you don't want to come out here, can I come in there? Please? *Please*?"

Mr. Jones got up, yanked the door open, and stuck his head outside. "What's wrong this time?" he asked, glaring at Mr. Smith.

Mr. Smith stood only inches from the door, facing outward with his back pressed against the building. He looked as if he had been frozen in place, except that he was shaking and sweating. His face was turned toward the door, his eyes fixed on Mr. Jones. His mouth moved, but no sound came out. His eyes shifted back and forth between Mr. Jones and something in front of the building. He looked like a very bad mime trying to silently convey a message.

It was clear that Mr. Smith was terrified...but of what? Mr. Jones tore his gaze away and turned to see what Mr. Smith was looking at. And then he saw...

Animals, all of them looking right at Mr. Smith and Mr. Jones. Not just a few animals, but an army of animals. It was like a scene from a war movie, but instead of soldiers and tanks, there were squads of raccoons, skunks, deer, squirrels, porcupines, and possums, all standing as if ready to march forward. Mr. Jones gawked at the assembled animals, dumbfounded.

"What the …?" he cried, but the crows, which started cawing non-stop, drowned out the last word.

All we heard was "Holy caw!" With that, I jumped up and ran straight at Mr. Jones. I pushed him with enough force to propel us both outside the building and onto the ground. Amy and Katie ran out the door right behind me, only to stumble over Mr. Jones and tumble down next to me.

It was a bizarre scene: Mr. Smith was pressed helplessly against the building, while Amy, Katie and I were sprawled on the ground just outside the door, and Mr. Jones was shaking his head, trying to gather his senses. We were all frozen in our places for a long moment, then Mr. Jones lifted his head, looked at me, and shouted, "Get the kids!"

I scrambled to my feet and yelled, "Run for it!"

I lunged at Mr. Jones, hoping to give Amy and Katie time to escape. They got up and ran toward the trees. Realizing that we were escaping jolted Mr. Smith into action. He was terrified of the animals, but he was even more afraid of Mr. Pickett's wrath. He started after Amy and Katie with a vengeance.

Mr. Jones was just getting up off the ground when I ran headlong into him. Boom! The collision sent both of us back to the ground.

Mr. Smith was gaining on Amy and Katie. He had just caught hold of Katie's shirt when the first wave of animals came to the rescue. He was yelling, "I got you! Come here!" when the raccoons launched their attack.

They went for Mr. Smith's legs, jumping against him and holding on until he could hardly move. He began to scream and shake his legs, trying to throw the raccoons off. That was when the squirrels joined the attack. They ran up his legs and started clawing and biting their way up his back, making their way toward his head.

Mr. Smith started screaming, "Help me! Help me!"

He fell to the ground but kept his grip on Katie, so she fell with him. Amy ran back to help Katie. She tried to pull Katie free as Mr. Smith jerked around on the ground, covered with raccoons and squirrels, but he hung on to Katie as if his life depended on it. Katie struggled and Amy pulled as hard as she could, but they were afraid to hit or kick Mr. Smith for fear they would injure the squirrels and raccoons so they all just wiggled back and forth in a big squirming heap.

The force of my collision had only stunned Mr. Jones for a moment. It had given Amy and Katie a chance to run, but now I was in his grasp. *Now what?* I thought. Mr. Jones was much bigger and heavier than I was. How could I break free?

Before we could get up off the ground, the foxes and rabbits came to my rescue. The foxes started biting Mr. Jones anywhere they could reach him, and the rabbits used their strong back legs to kick him in the face. I was amazed. Not only were animals rescuing me, but these mortal enemies were fighting together!

Mr. Jones started yelling, "Get them off! Get them off of me!" as the foxes and rabbits continued their attack. But although he was yelling, he managed to keep his tight grip on me.

The beavers were making their way toward the battle when a dirty, bitten, furious Mr. Jones managed to stand up and yell, "I've got the kid! Now get off of us or I'll hurt him!"

Mr. Jones grabbed me by the neck and jerked me to my feet. The next thing I knew, I was suspended in mid-air with his hands around my neck, gagging and in very big trouble. The action stopped.

"I will hurt the kid if you don't call off this madness!" Mr. Jones repeated, looking around with a menacing glare. "Whoever you are, call this off!" He searched for whoever might be the leader of this unlikely group of rescuers.

Mr. Smith struggled to his feet with Katie still in his clutches. He was looking at Katie and then got this weird look on his face. With his empty hand he began to pat his pants as if he was trying to find something. He was patting one leg and then the other. Then he abruptly stopped. He reached down his pants and pulled out a squirrel that, apparently had found its way up his pants leg. "Get out of there!" he yelled and tossed the squirrel away. Amy backed out of his reach, but stayed close.

The two men stood and faced the crowd of motionless animals. Their clothes were torn, caked with dirt, and soaked in animal saliva. They were panting and wild-eyed. But their confidence was returning now that they had the upper hand.

Mr. Smith demanded, "Who's in charge?" and tried to act like he was in control of the situation.

Mr. Jones looked around at the huge crowd of animals, still holding me suspended by my neck. "What's going on here?" he growled. He didn't have to act - it was obvious that he was in control.

"Take us to your leader," Mr. Smith commanded. Mr. Jones looked at him in complete disgust.

"We are taking the kids and *we are* leaving." Mr. Jones began, and then paused.

He kept me suspended as he moved cautiously toward Mr. Smith, who had a tight grip on Katie's shoulders. You could see from the expression on Mr. Jones' face that he was trying to apply logic to what was happening but couldn't figure out how to reason with a bunch of animals. He tried anyhow. "Whoever you are, we are taking the kids and we will hurt them if you try anything."

The men looked toward the building and realized that the animals had blocked their path. Taking refuge in the building was no longer an option.

Mr. Smith said, "Where are we going to go? There is a lot of woods out here."

"I don't have any idea. Just try to scare them."

"Don't try anything, or the kid gets it," Mr. Smith said, sounding like he was in a bad movie.

Mr. Jones rolled his eyes and told Mr. Smith, "That's enough, just shut up. That's not what I meant by scaring them."

Mr. Smith whined, "I just don't want them to bite me anymore. I don't think I could stand it if I got bitten even one more time."

The two men stood together, back to back, holding Katie and me like body shields and staring down the animals. As they wondered what to do next, their attention was drawn to a nearby bush. The bush, which was about fifteen yards from them, had begun to shake. The shaking slowly intensified. Then the bush began to glow with a faint light. The light grew in intensity until the entire bush radiated a brilliant blue light. Gradually, the light subsided.

The two men, Amy, Katie and I, and all of the animals stared at the bush. A creature walked slowly out into the open, then stopped and looked at us.

The animals knew what it was.

I knew what it was.

Amy knew what it was.

Katie thought she knew what it was.

Mr. Jones and Mr. Smith had never seen such an animal and didn't want to know what it was.

It was Sarah the Schmooney, in her natural state.

She had the back legs of a bobcat, the front legs of a black bear, the camouflage markings of a brown-tailed deer, and the face of a raccoon. The fur on her back was the thick coat of a skunk, her ears were those of a rabbit, and her tail was that of a beaver.

Sarah sent, *'Don't you dare harm them!'* It thundered through my body so loudly that it seemed impossible that not everyone could hear it.

Mr. Smith screamed, "It's a Pond Mutant!" and abruptly dropped Katie. Amy grabbed Katie's hand and they ran for the woods.

Mr. Jones was frozen in shock. He heard his pal's scream and turned to stare at him. His grip on my neck loosened slightly. He seemed dazed by this latest turn of events. I took as deep a breath as I could manage and kicked him in the side with all my strength. He dropped me to the ground. I fell in a heap.

Sarah saw that I was free. I heard her send, *'Get them!'* Without hesitation, the animals attacked.

I scrambled to my feet and ran after Katie and Amy. Mr. Jones and Mr. Smith did not do so well.

The raccoons and the squirrels leaped at Mr. Smith, knocking him to the ground again. Foxes and rabbits set upon Mr. Jones, and this time the beavers joined in. The skunks and a porcupine moved in to do their share. Mr. Smith had grabbed one of the raccoons around the neck. The porcupine smacked his quills into his thighs and rear end. With a great cry of pain he released the raccoon.

The groundhogs were rapidly approaching Mr. Jones. He saw their sharp teeth and claws and the speed at which they were approaching. He fought to get to his feet.

Mr. Smith was flat on the ground, with squirrels and raccoons all over his arms and legs to hold him down. Several skunks were backing toward his face. Mr. Smith looked up just in time to see them and screamed a helpless, "Nooooooo!" The skunks released their pungent odor directly into his face.

Mr. Jones had made it to his feet, and was shaking the remaining foxes off his legs. He looked up and realized that there were dozens of large animals coming toward them like a moving wall. When he saw the bears, that was just too much for him.

He yelled, "I'm getting out of here!" Then he turned, and immediately tripped over a battered Mr. Smith, landing on top of him. They struggled to separate their tangled limbs and get up as the wave of groundhogs, bears, and deer approached rapidly. At last the men made it to their feet. They looked around wildly. They didn't know where they would be safe, but they knew they had to get away from us. They took off, running as fast as they could, in the opposite direction from Amy, Katie and me.

That took them straight toward the pond. They ran into it without even slowing down and started swimming toward the relative safety of the middle, hoping the animals would not follow them into deep water.

Amy, Katie, and I ran until we reached the safety of the woods, then looked back to watch the end of the battle. Our former captors were treading water, looking fearfully around for attackers. It occurred to me that if the fish and frogs in the pond hadn't all been killed or driven away by the contamination, even the pond might not have offered escape from Sarah's army of devoted friends.

We heard Mr. Smith asking, "How long do you think we'll have to tread water?"

"As long as it takes for those killer animals to leave," Mr. Jones snarled.

We heard Mr. Smith's voice again, complaining as usual. "Yuck! This water smells awful."

We could just hear Mr. Jones retort, "Not as awful as you do. You stink!"

Chapter 11

The animals had come to our rescue and saved us. Amy, Katie, and I grinned and hugged each other. There were so many emotions flying through me that I could scarcely sort them out, but relief and astonishment were high on the list. We looked back again, surveying the battlefield.

The animals were separating into groups, mostly staying with their own kind. Some were beginning to slip away from the field to rejoin their family groups. Others were settling in to stand guard around the pond.

Amy and Katie were standing at the edge of the trees, watching the animals as they made their way into the woods. Katie was saying, "Thank you, Mr. Squirrel. Thank you, Mr. Raccoon."

As I watched the animals form a protective barrier around the pond it reminded me of the legend of the Schmooney. In the story, the animals had surrounded the exhausted hero so he could rest safely after saving them from what had threatened them. Here, the animals were surrounding the men who had threatened us, so we could leave safely. It was very strange, like being in the middle of a fairy tale that was still being written.

Suddenly, I realized that I had not seen Sarah since the beginning of the final attack. I scanned the field, searching for the bush where we had last seen her. When I located the bush, I saw her lying on the ground nearby. She wasn't moving. I hurried toward her, going as fast as I could, but keeping a respectful distance from the other animals.

As I approached Sarah the Schmooney, revealed in her fantastic natural state, she lay there motionless. *Sarah, poor brave Sarah,* I thought. Words were shouting in my head as I approached her, but I did not speak. *Don't leave me Sarah! Please, please don't leave me!*

As I reached her side I heard, *'See, I knew you could send without speaking.'* The message Sarah sent was weak, but she sounded satisfied.

I bent down and carefully picked up her limp body, cradling her in my arms.

'Hey, take it easy,' she sent.

'Are you hurt?' I sent back.

'When I change that fast it takes a lot of my energy. I am not hurt, just very tired and a bit sore.'

Amy and Katie walked over to us. "Is Sarah all right?" asked Amy.

"Yes," I reassured Amy and Katie. "Sarah is fine, but exhausted. She needs to rest."

"Thank goodness she's unharmed," Amy said, then spoke directly to Sarah. "Thank you, Sarah, for being so very brave, and for asking your animal friends to protect us. We will always remember what you did."

Amy fell silent, thinking about the amazing things that had happened since our morning began. Then she shook herself, as if awakening from a dream.

"Austin, Katie, let's not forget that we aren't done here," Amy said. "We've had an amazing escape, but we still have a big problem. We must get to the town meeting, but we don't have a car."

Some of the animals began to gather around Sarah. They instinctively knew that she had been weakened by her efforts and needed their protection. Katie was still trying to thank each of the animals, saying politely, "Thank you, Mr. Fox. Thank you, Mr., uh, Mr....." She stopped. "What is that?" she whispered loudly, pointing toward one of the animals.

"That's a groundhog, Katie," Amy told her.

"Oh. Thank you, Mr. Groundhog," Katie said.

Sarah sent, *'Austin, it's the pond. The pond is full of poison. There are barrels of poison up in a mountain cave. Other barrels like them have been poured into the pond. After heavy rains, the pond overflows into the stream that feeds the lake. Now even the lake is beginning to suffer.'*

I told Amy, "We need to take a sample of the pond water with us to show the town. We can use one of those Mason jars we saw in the shed."

"I'll get a sample of the water," Amy agreed, "and then we need to leave. Remember that we don't have a car, and we don't have a clue what they did with our compass and other equipment. It won't be easy to get back to town in time for the meeting."

Amy backtracked to the shed for a jar, then walked toward the pond. The animals standing guard moved aside to open a path for her. She filled the jar halfway with water from the pond. Mr. Jones and Mr. Smith glared at her, but didn't try to cause any more trouble. The animals allowed Amy to pass back through, then closed their circle again.

I sent, *'Sarah, will you come with us? I can carry you.'*

'No, I am too tired,' she sent. *'You will need to do this on your own. I will ask one of my friends to lead you through the forest. That way is shorter than the road, but still you will have to hurry.'*

Amy had returned with the water sample. She and Katie were standing next to me, waiting.

I found a soft bed of pine needles and carefully laid Sarah on it. *'You really are a Schmooney,'* I sent. *'This is so cool.'* I closed my eyes for a moment and stroked her gorgeous, multicolored fur.

Sarah sent, *'I just need time to rest, and then I will meet you at your house.'*

Amy said, "Austin, we need to go. Come on."

"I'm coming," I said, then got up and walked toward the woods. I glanced back. Sarah was lying comfortably in the field and the other animals were completing their circle around her. I smiled, thinking how much this resembled the story.

When we reached the woods we discovered the guide Sarah had arranged for us was a large, proud buck. The buck was magnificent. I had never seen such a beautiful animal, and to be so close was breathtaking. I stroked him lightly, my fingertips barely touching his side.

'Let's go,' I sent, not really knowing whether I could communicate with the buck, but figuring it was worth a try. As we started walking, the buck moved ahead of us into the woods. We followed our guide; me first, followed by Katie, and then Amy.

Amy commented, "Austin, it looks like you can now send without speaking out loud. Congratulations."

"Yea, wow, that's right, I didn't notice. Sarah told me that my communication skills would develop. It appears they have. But there's so much more to learn."

Amy looked at the Mason jar of pond water she was carrying. "There is definitely more to learn," she agreed.

What a day.

* * * * *

It was late afternoon. Final preparations for that night's town meeting were underway. The meeting room in Town Hall had an occupancy permit for just over 100 people, sitting and standing. That night's meeting was sure to attract a larger crowd than the room could hold. The mayor of Mountview, the Honorable Lewis Crest, had sent a crew to Town Hall to set up extra chairs in the hallway.

Mr. Pickett was walking through town on his way to Town Hall. He had just left the White House Restaurant, where a few hours earlier, he had entertained some of the town's more influential citizens at an elegant luncheon. He was pleased with the way that had turned out. Several of the community leaders had stayed afterward to talk about business opportunities that would result from the building project. He believed that he had been very effective in ensuring their support for the project. Nevertheless, he didn't want to miss this opportunity to stroll through downtown and make an effort to personally sway the opinion of anyone who might still be undecided.

"Good afternoon, Mrs. Berry," he said politely as he passed the hardware store.

"Hi," said the efficient Mrs. Berry, glancing up, then going back to what she was doing.

"Is your husband around?" Mr. Pickett inquired.

"No," she replied, and walked back into the store.

Mr. Pickett, like everyone else in town, was accustomed to Mrs. Berry's abbreviated conversations. He knew there was no point in stopping there. She wouldn't stay in one place long enough to listen to whatever he might want to say. He continued his walk toward Town Hall. He passed by Laura Dean's dress shop. He noticed the poster in the window. He stopped and starred at the poster. *I hate that kid,* he thought, then resumed his walk.

Dr. and Mrs. Dixon were just locking the front door of their house as they headed for Town Hall. The Town Council members planned to arrive early to make certain they would all be in place, seated at the front table, well before the meeting started.

Mrs. Dixon was excited. She knew that Mountview community was going to make a major decision tonight that would help shape the future of their town. What she didn't know was that it would be a decision that she would not be prepared for.

Uncle Steve had driven home from his meeting and discovered that Amy and the kids still weren't back from their early morning mission. He was worried about them. *Some guardian you are,* he thought to himself. *You've had them in your house for only a few days and already they're missing.*

"They aren't missing," he said out loud as he opened a bag of dog food and fed Edison. Patting Edison on the head, he said, "Don't worry, boy," as if it was the dog that needed to be reassured. "They're fine. I'm sure they're just off doing something silly."

* * * * *

Amy, Katie and I weren't doing something silly at all. We were walking as fast as we could through the forest. By this time, Amy was carrying Katie, who was very tired from the long day. I was so hot that I had removed my camouflaged shirt and tied it around my waist.

We followed the buck, on and on and on. We felt like we had been walking forever. I watched the buck glide through the brush and wondered how he could move so much more easily than we could. He would trot ahead, keeping just within our sight. Then he would pause, sniff the air, and listen for danger.

We needed water. We could hear the stream up ahead. Though we could not see it yet, we were relieved that rest and water were near. We began to move faster, eager to reach the stream.

*   *   *   *   *

Mr. Pickett was now passing through the courtyard area of the town, where the candy store was located.

"Hello, Mr. Bivens. Hello, Mrs. Steele." he said in his most pleasant voice.

He greeted everyone he knew by name, knowing that individual recognition would please them. He was working the owners and patrons of the local shops.

"Business is good, but business could always be better," he continued, attempting to gather support for his cause. "I'll see you at the town meeting, where what we're planning will help you build your business." Mr. Pickett was smiling, appearing to have a sincere interest in the welfare of his fellow citizens.

It was a comfortable feeling, knowing that his greatest adversary would not be at the meeting. How that little kid was able to motivate his opponents was interesting. Knowing that he had the boy safely locked up was like cheating in a card game, and, oh, how he loved to cheat in a card game. He continued to smile. Tonight, his smile was a real one. The deck was stacked.

Some of the shop owners had closed their businesses to get an early dinner. They didn't want to sit through a long, heated meeting without anything in their stomachs. Montgomery Simms took a handful of brochures with him as he closed the Simms Real Estate office. He wanted to be prepared. As soon as it was clear that the building plan would be supported, he would pass out the brochures and start taking orders. He could hear Mr. Berry saying, "The early bird gets the worm."

Billy Johnson had already arrived at Town Hall. He had put new Eveready batteries in his tape recorder and tucked his note pad into the pocket of his shirt. He knew it was pointless to be early, but he had wanted to secure a seat right up front. He passed the time before the meeting daydreaming about winning a Pulitzer Prize.

*   *   *   *   *

Uncle Steve was looking for a parking place on Main Street. He could see that the town meeting had already attracted a great many people since the closest available space was two blocks away. While he searched for a parking space, he was also searching for Amy's Suburban. It was nowhere to be seen. He got out of his Jeep, locked the doors, and looked at his watch. *6:45. Where are they?* he asked himself. He looked up and down Main Street. No sign of them. He glanced into the window of one of the shops on Main. He saw the poster, which caused him to smile. *Leave it to Austin*, he thought. As he turned, he waved as Mr. Gaines drove by, then walked in the direction of Town Hall.

Harvey Gaines parked his car a few spaces away. He quickly got out and looked for Uncle Steve, but he was already halfway down the block. Mr. Gaines considered calling out to get his attention, but decided to wait until they were both inside the Hall. Turning back to the car, he sorted through his papers until he located a very interesting piece of information that he wanted to bring up during the meeting. He placed that document in his briefcase, secured the clasp, and locked his car.

* * * * *

Katie was now walking on her own, but she was lagging behind. Our pace was too fast for her shorter legs. She would walk for a bit, fall far behind, run a little to catch up, then walk some more to catch her breath, and then run again to catch up.

After a final burst of speed Katie stopped in her tracks, completely winded, and gasped, "I can't walk anymore."

Amy and I stopped. "What time is it?" I asked.

I was winded, too, but when I saw how totally exhausted Katie looked I didn't have the heart to complain. The forest was getting darker. I looked through the trees, trying to see how low the sun was. Our trip was going to become a lot more difficult once it was dark.

Amy voiced what I was thinking. "It will be dark very soon. We need to keep going."

Amy thought about what to do. She knew how tired she was. She looked at Katie and realized that Katie really couldn't walk any longer. She was too tired to carry Katie anymore, and she could tell that I was too tired to carry her. What could we do? She looked for answers.

The big buck stood nearby. All day long we had followed him, watching closely but not wanting to crowd him. He would glide silently through the trees, then something would catch his attention and he would stop, listen, and sniff the air, standing very still as if he were a statue. In different circumstances, it would be magnificent to watch.

Amy watched him test the air for scents when she got an idea. She extended her arm, keeping her hand open and relaxed, and walked slowly toward the buck. His body didn't move, but his head turned toward Amy's approaching figure.

Chapter 12

The Town Hall chairs had found occupants. If you wanted to be in the meeting room, you had to stand. People were still coming into the room, checking to see if chairs were available, then deciding whether to stand or take a seat in the hallway outside the room. Posters were brought in by several of the townspeople and placed at various spots in the hall. Mrs. Dixon and the other members of the Town Council were seated at the front table, facing the crowd. Harvey Gaines was one of the people standing along the walls. He had lost sight of Uncle Steve.

The sound of the gavel pounding the table echoed throughout the hall. Mr. Lewis Crest, the mayor of Mountview, was calling the meeting to order.

"This special meeting of, and for, Mountview community is now officially in session," the mayor announced, tapping his gavel on the table for a final time. He looked solemnly around the crowded room.

"First, I will ask Mrs. Dixon to read the order of business that we will discuss tonight. Keep in mind that we will use the 'Mountview version' of Parliamentary Procedure. What that means is that no one speaks unless I acknowledge them. In order to control this meeting, I have the authority to cut off anyone at any time. If you do not do what I say, then the sheriff here..." His voice trailed off. "Pete, where are you?" Mayor Crest looked around the room until he spotted Sheriff Pete Hawkins. "Oh, there you are." He pointed to the sheriff standing at the back of the room, then continued. "If you do not do what I say, the sheriff will remove you from the premises.

"OK, first the Council will present an overview of the proposal that has been presented for consideration. Then the party requesting the approval, Mr. DeWitt Pickett, will be given time to speak. The other interested parties will be given an opportunity to speak after that, beginning with Ms. Amy Bryant, who submitted a formal request to speak. We are limiting this meeting to one hour so that we won't be here all night. The Town Council and I," he said, glancing down the table at the rest of the Council members, "will make a decision no later than tomorrow at noon. Is that clear?" He paused and looked around the room. "All right then, is Mr. DeWitt Pickett present?"

Mr. Pickett rose to his full height and said, "Yes, Mr. Mayor, Mr. DeWitt Pickett is present." He sat down.

"All right then, is Ms. Amy Bryant present?" The mayor looked around the room. There was no response. The audience looked around the room, expecting to hear Amy's voice. Silence. Someone in the hallway called out, "She's not out here!" There was scattered laughter. Mayor Crest said, "Well, I'm sure she will be here any time now.

"Remember, we will close the meeting by 8:30 sharp. That should give all sides a chance to present their views." He stopped and looked around the room, then turned to look at Mrs. Dixon. "Mrs. Dixon, would you please present an overview of the proposal?"

Mrs. Dixon stood and began to address the crowded room. "Mountview Town Council has received a proposal for construction of a fifteen-story condominium, to be built on the south side of Sunset Rock." She pointed to a clearly marked area on a map that was resting on an easel next to her, angled so everyone could see, then continued. "The proposed project will…"

* * * * *

With the sun just above the western horizon, the thick brush and the heavy concentration of oak trees blocked nearly all of the remaining light. Twilight had fallen on Amy, Katie and me. Amy was trailing slightly behind us, looking around for something familiar, but with the growing darkness, visibility was limited. She thought the buck was taking us to town, but he was taking a route unfamiliar to her.

I had not been able to communicate with the buck. That frustrated me. I was also unable to communicate with Sarah. That worried me. Amy reassured me, suggesting that perhaps Sarah was too tired, or perhaps we were out of range. "Who knows why?" she asked, not really expecting an answer. "There's so much more to learn about that. Don't worry. Sarah has recovered from much worse injuries. Remember the fire? She will be fine; she's just very tired."

I was walking directly behind the buck, having a hard time keeping up. It was so dark now that when we walked through areas of heavy brush, it was easy to lose sight of the buck. I was fascinated to see how easily the buck's grayish brown coat blended into the shadows of the darkening forest. The only thing that enabled me to stay close was that Katie was humming. And the only thing making that possible was that Katie was now riding the buck. Amazing.

"How come *she* gets to ride the buck?" I had asked when we heard Amy's idea. But I had already known the answer. Perhaps when all of this was over I would get my turn. For now, we had one goal – to get to town before the meeting was over.

* * * * *

"Thank you, Mrs. Dixon, for a very thorough presentation," Mayor Crest said. He glanced at his watch and made a mental note of the time remaining – forty-five minutes. "Now we will have our first speaker. Mr. DeWitt Pickett, would you please stand at the podium?"

Mr. Pickett rose, walked to the front of the room, and took his place behind the podium. He let his gaze sweep slowly across the audience and then began to speak.

"Thank you, Mr. Mayor. I am DeWitt Pickett. I am a developer and the owner of a rather large parcel of land here in and around Mountview. I am here tonight to talk to you from two different perspectives. The first perspective is that of a concerned citizen protecting our community and building for a better tomorrow. The second perspective is that of a business owner and a Mountview property owner. In those roles I, just like many of you, am encouraged to profit from my investments and from a lifetime of hard work.

"Concerning the first perspective, I am on the Board of Directors of this proposed building project and have witnessed first hand the countless hours we have spent carefully reviewing the plans to ensure that our beloved community will not be harmed. We want to preserve our treasured land. We also want to provide a historical reminder of our treasured past, which we will do by erecting a monument that will allow many, not just a few, to witness what nature has bestowed upon us.

"Now, let's look at the condominium itself." Mr. Pickett placed a large architect's drawing of the building and site on the easel near the podium. He gestured toward various features as he spoke. "Do you see how we are building with nature, not opposed to her? You can see, and I am certain that you will agree, that our natural setting will remain safe and will be preserved.

"Now, for the second perspective. Many of us here today own land in Mountview, and many of us here today have built businesses that are located in the town of Mountview; land and businesses that we will pass on to our families to preserve our personal heritage. But how is this guaranteed? It is not. We can only preserve our way of life as long as we have the income we need to support our property and businesses.

"How do we plan to do that? There are so many uncertainties. This building project offers you the best guarantees you will ever receive. It will bring the community one hundred fifty new families, translating to more customers and thus additional income to help you ensure the continued success of your businesses. It will drive a stronger, more stable economy, which will keep property values high and help each of us protect our personal investment in the community. As you can see, what we are really creating is not just a building. What we are creating is a more prosperous community, one that will be permanently improved by these changes. Can you think of anything else that would do more to protect the future for you and your family?

"In summary, my opponents…wherever they are…want to talk about the evils of development. We are not here tonight to discuss development. You know it and I know it; development will come to Mountview. If it isn't today, it will be tomorrow. But if it happens tomorrow, when we are gone, then we can't control it. If we don't control it, then we are controlled by it. And if that happens, you could lose your business, your land, and your heritage.

"Now is the time for the Mountview community to build. Before the outsiders build. We will build our way, the right way, and preserve nature. Ladies and gentlemen, as my father used to say, 'The future is for those who embrace it.' So please, for the sake of your own futures, embrace this building project."

Mr. Pickett paused dramatically, looking around the room. "Now I ask you, what do think about a beautiful new building, right here in Mountview?"

There was a thunderous round of applause. Mr. Pickett stood, basking in the attention. Ah, how he loved being in the spotlight.

*   *   *   *   *

"I can hear a car, we're finally there!" Katie cried out.

Amy heard it, too. Then she saw a glimmer of artificial lights off in the distance. She started to move ahead of us so she could get her bearings. But the path was narrow, and it was now quite dark. As Amy tried to pass me, her foot slipped on an unseen rock and she stumbled. I lunged toward her and was able to grab her right arm, but it was too little, too late. She fell hard on her left side. Unfortunately, that was the side where she was carrying the glass Mason jar containing pond water. The jar shattered, splashing part of its contents onto her clothes but most of them onto the forest floor. The broken glass scattered too, but some of it lodged in Amy's rib cage where she had fallen directly on top of it.

"Oh, no," Amy groaned. With her right hand she searched for the source of the pain. Her fingers felt the cool thin liquid of the water on her wet clothes, but that was quickly replaced with a thicker, warmer liquid. Blood.

Katie slid off of the buck. I knelt down to determine how bad Amy's cuts were. I could barely see, but it was clear she was in quite a bit of pain.

"You can't continue," I told Amy. "You need to stay here. Katie, stay with Amy. I'll go get some help."

"No, Austin, I can make it," she insisted.

"You might make it to the meeting, but you wouldn't do much else. Amy, sometimes life itself becomes more important than the plans we make in our lives. Now, please…stay here and I'll get some help."

I jumped up, and, driven by adrenalin, ran toward the lights of the town.

* * * * *

"Thank you, Mr. Pickett," Mayor Crest said. "Now we will hear from Ms. Amy Bryant. Ms. Bryant, are you here?"

Uncle Steve stood up and said, "Ms. Bryant has been delayed, but will be arriving soon. She respectfully requests permission to present her comments at the last part of the meeting, to close the meeting."

"So are you saying that Ms. Bryant wants to be the last presenter? I don't see anything wrong with that," the mayor responded. "But let me remind you that time is about up."

"Yes, sir," Uncle Steve replied. He walked quickly from the room and left the meeting in search of Amy.

"Do I have any requests from the floor?" Mayor Crest asked. The room came to life with voices wanting to be heard.

"Steve! Steve!" Mr. Gaines called to Uncle Steve. But Mr. Gaines was stuck against the wall and the crowd was noisy. He was unable to get Uncle Steve's attention before he left.

Mr. Gaines raised his hand and said, "Mr. Mayor, I have something to say." But before he could catch the mayor's eye, Mr. Simms had permission to speak and was walking to the podium.

* * * * *

Uncle Steve paused outside the building and looked both ways. He decided to walk west, since it was the closest to where Amy had headed for the day. He started out walking fast and then broke into a run. He had passed through several lights when he heard someone yelling. It was a familiar voice. It was me.

* * * * *

Mr. Simms was finishing his comments on the building project. Nothing new. He wanted to sell property; everyone knew that. The floor was opened again.

104

Mr. Gaines once again started yelling, "Mr. Mayor! Mr. Mayor!" But he wasn't recognized.

"The floor recognizes Mr. Berry."

With that, Mr. Gaines threaded his way through the standing-room-only crowd, which was now packed like sardines since the people who had been in the hallway had moved into the meeting room in order to see and hear the action better. Mr. Gaines left the meeting room, closing the doors behind him, to go in search of Uncle Steve who was probably the only person who would recognize the urgency of what Mr. Gaines had to say.

*　*　*　*　*

But Uncle Steve was several blocks away, rushing toward me. "Uncle Steve!" I yelled, running into his waiting arms.

"Where have you been? Where are Amy and Katie? I've been so worried!"

"They're right past the post office, in the woods. Amy is hurt. She fell down. She's OK, but she's bleeding and needs your help. Katie is with her."

"OK, I'll go find them," Uncle Steve told me. "Where are you going?"

"We know where the water is being poisoned. I need to tell the town. If you will take care of Amy, I'll take care of business. I'm going to Town Hall."

"OK, Austin, I'll take care of Amy and Katie. But you're nearly out of time. We both need to hurry." He shook his head and an odd look appeared on his face, as if suddenly registering my condition. "Boy, do you stink! Did you have a close encounter with a skunk?"

"I'll explain later!" I called, running toward Town Hall. I knew that Amy would be fine. I wasn't too sure if my clothes would ever be the same. I must have gotten some of the spray from the skunks when they sprayed. But that was too bad. There was no time to change.

I ran through the open front door, past Mr. Gaines. I ran down the hall, with Mr. Gaines right behind me, towards the doors that separated me from the meeting. I was running so fast that I couldn't stop in time. I was nearly out of control and about to fall over when I slammed into the doors. The doors flew open, fortunately not hitting anyone standing inside, and I tumbled onto the floor of the hall.

My grand entrance stopped the meeting and attracted the attention of everyone in the room, including Mr. DeWitt Pickett. His eyes were wide open as he stood to get a better look at me lying on the floor. I knew he must be wondering, *'How did **he** get here?'* I also knew he didn't think anyone would believe me. He looked like he was fighting to stay calm. But it was almost time for the meeting to end and who was going to believe a kid. He found his control and so he remained calm.

Mr. Berry had just finished his presentation when I came tumbling in. Mayor Crest was staring at me, as was everyone else. The mayor said, "Austin, do you have anything to add?"

I was stunned from hitting the doors so hard. I was looking at about a hundred people who were all staring back at me. Silence had filled the room.

"Ah, hello, Mr. Mayor. I'm sorry for barging in." I was trying to stand up. I began to brush off my clothes and noticed how dirty I was. Oh well, it didn't seem to be much use, so I stopped. "Yes, Mr. Mayor, I do have something to say. Do I have time?" I asked as I walked towards the front of the room.

"Actually, you do. It seems that Ms. Bryant is not here to present her side, so maybe you can speak for her." The mayor motioned for me to approach, "Come up here and say what's on your mind."

I walked to the front of the room. Everyone I passed was responding to my smell, covering their noses and making faces as they caught a whiff of the unpleasant scent.

I began by stating the obvious. "I apologize for the way I look…and smell. I had a close encounter with a skunk." I cleared my throat since it was beginning to get dry. "I know you have heard a lot about all of this already. I know that I have. But please hear me out.

"Since Mr. Pickett has already spoken, I'm sure he has told you that this building project would be good for the environment. He claims that it's important to make money. He is a good speaker so he probably has convinced many of you to agree with him. I'm not here to change your

106

mind. I am only a kid – what do I know? You have worked hard for what you have; you deserve to benefit from that.

"If Mr. Berry were up here, he would probably say something like this." I remembered what Mom told me. It seemed like the perfect thing to say. "'Behavior is how you act when everyone is watching. Character is how you act when no one is watching.' Mr. Pickett's behavior has fooled us all into believing he is a man who wants to help us. But his character is telling us the real truth, and the truth is that Mr. Pickett is not a very nice man. In fact, he is downright mean." I noticed that Mr. Picket was sitting off to the left. I avoided looking in his direction and continued.

"Amy wanted to be here tonight, but she cut herself bringing you a glass jar of water from Mr. Pickett's pond. She was bringing that water to show you that it is full of poison." I looked over the front table. I saw Mrs. Dixon who was listening intently. "That pond is polluting our water. Mr. Pickett knows it. He wants to use the building project to cover this up. If you side with him and let this pass, your children will pay for your mistake."

The crowd erupted. Everyone started talking at once. The mayor began to pound his gavel, trying to get the meeting back under control.

"Mr. Mayor? Mr. Mayor, I demand to be recognized!" Mr. Pickett shouted over the noise of the crowd.

"Yes, Mr. Pickett," the mayor said, after the noise quieted down some. "You can stand where you are and be recognized. Do you have a response?"

"Yes, Mr. Mayor, I certainly do," Mr. Pickett said. "I am shocked. I am insulted. This has gone far enough. This...little boy," he said looking at me scornfully and pointing, "is making gross misstatements that he can't possibly support. I cannot believe that you are permitting this type of, of, guerrilla tactics to tarnish the reputation of one of Mountview's most honored citizens. I will be forced to consider legal action."

Mayor Crest looked at me. "Austin, what you are saying is very damaging. Do you have any proof at all?"

"No sir, I don't. Except if you postpone this meeting long enough to go test the water at Mr. Pickett's' pond..."

"See what I'm telling you?" Mr. Pickett interrupted. "He has no proof. This is just a childish delay tactic. You are all being played for fools."

"Quiet, quiet, quiet!" the mayor ordered, banging his gavel. "Mr. Pickett, it is still Austin's turn to speak and I want to hear what he has to say." Mr. Pickett slowly sank into his chair.

Mayor Crest looked back at me. "Austin, if you have no proof, then what can we do? I am afraid that I must ask you to sit down."

I was out of things to say. I knew the mayor was right. It looked like I lost. That very moment, a huge weight landed right on my shoulders. I was beaten. My head fell and I just stood there and stared at the floor.

The mayor addressed the audience and the other Town Council members. "Since we are now out of time, I will entertain a motion to close this meeting…"

"Wait, wait," said a familiar voice from the doorway. "I have something to say."

I looked up and searched the room to see who was speaking. I noticed Mr. Gaines waving a paper in his hand as he entered the room and walked through the crowded hallway.

"Mr. Mayor, the scheduled time has expired. I move that we end this meeting," Mr. Pickett said smoothly, as if he hadn't heard Mr. Gaines.

"Mr. Pickett, according to my watch, we still have one minute left in the meeting," the mayor answered. "The chair recognizes Mr. Gaines, who I hope has something important to say."

"Yes, Mr. Mayor, I believe I do." Mr. Gaines stood at the back of the room, facing the front. He raised the paper again and said, "I received this confirmation from the County just this afternoon that toxic chemicals have been discovered in Jackson Stream. As you know, Jackson Stream runs along the side of Pickett's pond. It is very possible that Austin is correct. Pickett's pond needs to be tested. It may be the source of pollutants."

The voices in the room reached a high level of noise as nearly everyone started talking.

Over the buzzing of voices I heard Mr. Picket yell, "I protest, Mr. Mayor! I object! This has nothing to do with the building project!"

"And I protest too, Mr. Pickett," said Mayor Crest, clearly beginning to lose his patience. "I protest that you are protesting. Sit down, Mr. Pickett," he ordered while pounding his gavel. "Sit down *now*! Sheriff?" He looked meaningfully at the sheriff, then back to Mr. Pickett. Mr. Pickett sat down again. "Council, do any of you wish to offer a motion?"

Mrs. Dixon spoke loud enough for the entire room to hear her. "I move that we suspend all discussions and considerations related to the proposed building project until we obtain the data necessary to investigate this claim and determine whether it is factual. Further, I move that we start obtaining that data first thing in the morning."

"I second that motion," said one of the other Town Council members.

Mayor Crest looked at the other Council members and said, "All in favor say 'Aye.'" There was a chorus of 'ayes,' and Town Hall responded with thunderous and resounding approval.

The mayor pounded his gavel to restore order. "Anyone opposed?" he asked the Council members.

The Council members were silent. Mr. Pickett was the lone person saying "Nay," and he didn't have the right to vote. The Council members quickly went through the process of officially ending the meeting.

The meeting was over. Everyone had known that this would be an important meeting, and most people had predicted that it would be a lively debate. But this outcome was not what anyone had expected. People were talking excitedly about what had happened. Little by little, people began to file out of the room.

The townspeople were relieved that the source of the water pollution had been tentatively identified. Many of them came over to me before they left the room. Some of then simply patted me on the back as they walked by. Others stopped to thank me. Most of them were holding their noses, but they came to see me anyhow.

The Town Council members had packed up their belongings and the room was gradually emptying. I spotted the sheriff. I decided to ask for a ride to the clinic, to make sure that Amy was all right. As I approached the sheriff, I could see that he was talking to Mr. Pickett, who was sitting down. Mr. Pickett didn't look so good. His head was in his hands as if he was getting some very bad news. Apparently, Sheriff Hawkins was planning to visit his property, specifically the pond, tomorrow. I wondered if Mr. Smith and Mr. Jones would be there, too. Suddenly, I chuckled, wondering if Mr. Smith and Mr. Jones would still be *in* the pond when the sheriff arrived.

Mr. Pickett looked up and noticed me standing behind the sheriff. The look he gave me was one that I had felt before. It was the same menacing look he had given me after we met on the street several days before. The hair on my neck seemed to tingle as if Mr. Pickett's look could penetrate my skin.

But this time, things were different. I returned the stare. I wasn't afraid any longer. I might be just a boy without his parents, far away from home, but I wasn't alone anymore. Mr. Pickett might be evil, but there was enough good out there to fight him.

Chapter 13

When we pulled up to Mountview Clinic, Uncle Steve's Jeep was in the parking lot. I thanked the sheriff for giving me a ride and he said goodbye. I mentioned to Sheriff Hawkins that I had a reason for being late to the meeting and I wanted to press charges against Mr. Picket. The sheriff agreed to meet with Amy and me tomorrow for us to tell him the whole story. I got out of his car. He watched until I walked to the door, turned and waved, then he drove away as I walked inside.

I found Katie and Uncle Steve in the small waiting room. Uncle Steve was sitting on a padded bench with Katie curled against him, sleeping.

"Austin," Uncle Steve said, "we've been waiting for you. We hoped you would come here."

His voice woke Katie. She blinked sleepily, then smiled and held out her arms to me. I knelt down and hugged her.

She said, "I told Uncle Steve about what happened today."

"That's good. How is Amy?" I asked.

Uncle Steve said, "She's fine. She's the proud owner of several stitches but she's fine. Doctor Preston wants to keep her here overnight. She did lose a lot of blood. They want to keep an eye on her until tomorrow just to be careful."

He put his hands on my shoulders and waited until I glanced up. He was looking into my eyes with a serious expression. "Austin, you did the right thing, making Amy stay where she was while you went to get help. If she had tried to walk into town she would have lost a lot more blood and things might not have ended so well. I'm proud of you for keeping your head and using your survival training when you were in an emergency situation. Thank you for taking care of Amy. You did very well."

I was pleased and proud and embarrassed all at the same time. I looked down, not sure what to say. Uncle Steve smiled, and changed the subject.

"So tell me, what happened at the town meeting?"

I quickly filled him in on what had happened.

"Well, we knew that meeting would be an interesting one, but I don't think anyone could have predicted all of this. It's been a wild day," Uncle Steve commented when I was done.

"Yeah, it sure has been a wild day," I agreed. "Can we go home now?"

"We sure can," Uncle Steve said. He helped Katie to her feet and we left.

The brief ride home was a blur. I may have slept, I really didn't remember. But the next thing I noticed was that we were pulling into the driveway.

When we got out of the car, Edison greeted us enthusiastically.

"Hey boy," I said. As usual, Edison approached me first. As we walked to the front door he kept rubbing against my leg. The faint moonlight made his dark fur gleam.

"Hey boy, you must really be lonely," I said, petting Edison. "Did you think we weren't coming back?"

We walked through the front door. Katie headed straight toward the stairs.

"Wait, wait," Uncle Steve called out to her, "Remember the skunks? You need to get cleaned up. Go take a bath and put on your pajamas, and then put your dirty clothes out on the deck. We'll deal with them tomorrow. You, too, Austin. You guys both need to take a bath before you go to bed."

"I was so tired, I forgot about how bad we must smell," I said. "Katie, leave your clothes by the bathroom door and I'll take them out with mine. You can take your bath first."

"Austin, after you get all the clothes on the deck, you can use my bathroom to take a shower," Uncle Steve told me.

I took off my dirty, smelly clothes while Katie was in the bathroom. I grabbed whatever was convenient: it was a swimsuit and a Georgia Tech T-shirt that were lying on top of my bed. I gathered up my dirty clothes, retrieved Katie's clothes from outside the bathroom door, and took the whole smelly bundle downstairs.

I walked outside and dropped the clothes on the deck. The night was cool and the insects were making their familiar nightly noises. I smelled the air, or at least tried to. The night air really didn't have a smell tonight. I decided that having the skunk odor so close by ruined my ability to smell anything else. I went back inside to take a shower in Uncle Steve's bathroom.

It was a brief shower, but a good one. I finally felt like I was getting back to normal. I walked out of the bathroom in my makeshift pajamas and saw Uncle Steve fast asleep in his bed with Edison curled up on top of the covers next to him. It must have been a tiring day for Uncle Steve, too.

I was quietly walking down the hall when I heard, *'Hey, where are you?'*

I was relieved to hear from Sarah. I stopped walking so I could concentrate on sending without talking out loud. *'I'm at the house. Where are you?'*

'I am at your house, too.'

'You are?' I sent, and started walking out the back door. *'Are you on the deck?'*

'No. I am sitting next to Katie.'

"Katie?" I said out loud, startled by the thought. *'But Katie is upstairs taking a bath,'* I sent.

'She is in her bed now, asleep.'

I ran toward the stairs, sending, *'I'm on my way up.'*

The bedroom door was open. I looked into the room. Katie was under the covers and apparently asleep. Right next to Katie, sitting on her bed, was Sarah. Not Sarah the Skunk. Not Sarah the Raccoon. But Sarah the Schmooney.

I stood there for a moment and just stared. A tired smile came across my face.

'Don't just stand there,' she sent, *'come over here; we have lots to talk about.'*

I walked over and, without thinking, sat on Katie's bed. The sudden weight of my body tilted the surface of the bed, causing Sarah to fall on top of Katie. The movement of the bed combined with Sarah falling on her caused Katie to stir and then wake up. She looked at me, and then she looked right at Sarah.

Oh no, I thought, *this is going to scare her.*

"Good night, Austin." She paused for a moment, put her hand out and petted Sarah, then said, "Good night, Edison." Then she turned toward the wall and went back to sleep.

I rubbed my head in amazement. Sarah sent, *'Let's sit on the floor.'*

I sent, *'I can't believe that I am looking at a Schmooney.'* I started petting her coat.

'A real live Schmooney,' she announced jokingly.

'There is so much to learn. Why are you a Schmooney now and not a skunk, or a raccoon? Why isn't Edison up here barking at you? Why did you almost die today? I was worried! Why...'

Sarah sent, *'Slow down, Austin, one at a time. First, yes, I have so much to tell you. I will tell you some tonight, but we are both tired and need some rest. We can talk again in the morning.*

'OK, here we go. I will try to explain how I change. I am here to protect the animals of the forest. In order for me to do that, I must be one of the animals **in** the forest. But some animals don't trust other ones, so how can I help them, when they won't let me get near them? You see, the skunks trust everyone but the owls, the rabbits don't trust the foxes, and no one trusts the squirrels. It is just like you humans. You have some groups of humans that don't trust other groups of humans, just because they are different. It's crazy. So the only way to capture everyone's trust is to be just like everyone. But the only way that can be done is through transformation. So I automatically transform to any creature that I am with at the time.'

'So, why aren't you a human right now? Since you're here with us, I mean.'

'Good question, Austin. It takes time for me to change. I have to be with the animals constantly for several days for me to change. If it didn't work that way, then I would walk through the forest and be changing like a traffic light.'

'That's another thing. How do you know things like traffic lights or my house?'

'When I change and pick up the features of the animal, I also pick up their language and their words.'

'So how were you able to change into a Schmooney today? This morning you were a raccoon,' I pointed out.

'That is another good question. I was so afraid you were going to be hurt that my emotions changed me immediately without warning. It took so much energy that I became exhausted.'

I was thinking about what she had said when I noticed a radiant blue light coming in through the window. My eyes widened. I turned to look at Sarah, to see if she saw the light, too. She looked back at me and sent, 'Oh, yes, I met a friend of yours today.'

'A friend of mine? Who was it?' I sent, without taking my eyes off the window.

'Well, she didn't say a lot to me, but she has something to tell you.' Sarah moved across the bed, onto the table and put her front bear paws

115

on the open window sill, while looking out over the deck. *'She is right out here, Austin."*

I got up and looked outside the open window. My arms were resting on the windowsill as I looked out over the back deck. Sarah sat next to me with her back legs on the table. My arms and her paws were side-by-side on the windowsill as we both looked outside.

There, standing on the back portion of the deck, was the Indian Princess. Her turquoise necklace was radiating a soft blue light that lit the entire backyard.

My eyes widened. "Princess," I whispered.

She spoke, "We needed you, Austin. We needed you to stop the poisoning. We needed you to stop the building on top of our burial ground. You have done that. My people thank you."

I stared, still amazed at what I was seeing and hearing. "Oh. It was nothing," I stammered. I looked over at Sarah, then looked back again to the Princess. "Well, maybe it was something."

The Princess continued, "I want to thank you for something even greater. You and Sarah have removed the curse that has haunted me for centuries. I can now rest in peace. I must leave now, but I will always be indebted to you. And don't ever forget, let nature takes its course," she said as the glow of the turquoise necklace slowly faded out. As the light faded, so did her image. And then she was gone.

I was still looking at the deck, in amazement, but now I saw nothing. I was lost in the day's events. Sarah was also staring out the window, deep in thought.

'Wow,' I sent as my gaze remained on the deck. *'What a day. My life was threatened, I have been held hostage, I have watched an army of animals save my life, I have had a deer as a guide, I talked to a three hundred-year-old Indian princess with a glowing necklace, and now I'm having a conversation with you.'* I looked at Sarah. *'An animal that changes its appearance like I change my shirt, a real live version of Name-That-Animal...what could possibly happen next?'*

I thought I heard Sarah laughing. I started to smile. *'So what's next?'* I sent.

Sarah looked back at me and sent, *'Who knows what will happen? Just let nature take its course.'*

We looked out the window, realizing how exciting things had become. I know that we shared the feeling that the adventure had just begun.

About the Author

Bob Shumaker was raised in Cuyahoga Falls, Ohio and now lives in Simpsonville, South Carolina with his wife, Sharon and their daughter, Katy. He retired early from his sales and marketing company to focus on one of his lifelong passions: writing. He began writing at age nine, inventing short stories and plays for his family and friends, and has never lost his love of storytelling. *The Spirit of the Turquoise Necklace* is Book Two of The Schmooney Trilogies, a series of fantasy adventure novels for children. Book One, *The Secret of the Enchanted Forest* is available at leading book sellers. Watch the website www.schmooney.com for news about his next books and other creative ventures,

Printed in the United States
29147LVS00006B/154-228

9 781420 851434